Ancient Prejudice, Break to New Mutiny...

Ancient Prejudice, Break to New Mutiny...

by Mark A. Roeder

toExcel

San Jose New York Lincoln Shanghai

Ancient Prejudice, Break to New Mutiny...

For information address:
toExcel
165 West 95th Street, Suite B-N
New York, NY 10025
www.toExcel.com

ISBN: 1-58348-206-7

Library of Congress Catalog Card Number: 99-61478

Printed in the United States of America

0 9 8 7 6 5 4 3 2 1

CONTENTS

"In fair Verona, where we lay our scene. From ancient grudge, break to new mutiny. Where civil blood makes civil hands unclean. From forth the fatal loins of these two foes, a pair of star crossed lover's take their life. Whose misadventures piteous overthrows, doth with their death bury their parents strife..."

That's as far as I'd made in on my English report, only a few short words copied directly from a tattered paperback. I crumpled the paper into a ball and sent it sailing toward the wastebasket. It dropped in with a satisfying thump. I wouldn't be needing it any more. Like my life, it had become unwanted and without reason for existence.

I'd struggled through Shakespeare, but I had come to understand him only too well. Life was a tragedy. When first I read "Romeo and Juliet", a task I undertook only under duress, I believed his work bore little resemblance to modern existence. Who really gave a damn about a four hundred year old romance? And why didn't Romeo just find some other babe to plow? My eyes had opened since that day however and I had grown. Shakespeare's words began to make sense. After the events of past few weeks, he could well have been telling the story of my own miserable life. "In fair Verona, Indiana, where we lay our scene. From ancient prejudice, break to new mutiny..."

The parallel was only too clear, but my story did not possess the romantic distance of a past age. The memory of what had so recently passed was not yet dulled and blurred by time. Centuries did not separate me from those terrible events. The wounds were not healed, but were still fresh and painful. Salt was yet being heaped upon them, sharpening the pain, intensifying the torment. My recent past was like a sharp stick, jabbing me in the gut, impaling me while I squirmed to escape. There could be no escape for me however, my fate was set.

All was lost. There was just no other way to describe it, everything that I cared about was gone. My mind reeled with sorrow. How could it all have come to such a pass? Why did it have to be this way? Why couldn't those around me have just understood and let me, let us, be?

Recording what had happened would be a time-consuming task, but I possessed the freedom of a doomed man. I had the rest of my life to set down what had happened. I felt an overpowering need to tell my story. I pulled the keyboard of the computer toward me and began my tale. I'd leave an account of what had happened, so maybe some other boy would not meet my fate.

1 The Boy of My Dreams

I first laid eyes on Taylor at a Thursday night high school dance. Usually all the dances were on the weekends, but sometimes they were through the week. I guess my school was just weird. I had never seen him before, without doubt, he was new. Our school wasn't so big that he could have escaped my notice, and there was no way I could have forgotten him. Others maybe, but never him. I couldn't take my eyes off Taylor. My gaze followed wherever he roamed. Usually I was far, far more cautious, one in my situation had to be, but for once I just stared. I couldn't help it. I had no control whatsoever, neither over my eyes, nor my heart.

I'd checked out guys before. I'd found myself looking at them with a distinct, almost painful yearning. Just before I'd spotted Taylor, I was gazing at a well muscled youth wearing a tight tank top. The knotted muscles in his arms and shoulders fed a hunger that sometimes threatened to devour me. Yes, I'd checked out guys before, but something stirred inside me, that had not stirred before. Here was the difference between hungering with the body and yearning with the soul. There was something about Taylor, something that drew me to him. My eyes had often been drawn to attractive young men, but never my heart, until the moment I laid eyes on him.

There was plenty to attract both my eyes and my heart. Taylor was, without doubt, the most beautiful boy I had ever beheld, but it was more than that, he radiated a kindness and cheerfulness that was so distinct, it was practically a visible phenomena. I felt myself drawn to him, as if by some irresistible force. I fell for him on the spot. With one look I was taken. What happened after was unimportant, from that first moment I was and always would be his. Somehow I knew it my heart it was true.

A boyfriend was the last thing I expected to find at a dance. I usually shied away from dances. It wasn't that I didn't like to dance, any sort of physical activity attracted me, it was something quite different. I was popular at school; athletic, good looking, just the sort of boy that drew girls to him without effort. That the was the problem - the girls. What would have been to most boys my age an opportunity; an arousing, exciting possibility, was to me a predicament. I feared girls as a vampire does the mirror. They were an instrument that could expose me for what I was.

I often thought of myself as a vampire. Like those mythical creatures of the night, I lived a secret life. I hid my true nature, protecting myself from those who could not, or would not, understand. I pretended to be just like my friends and classmates, but I was something vastly different from the boy they saw before them each day. I cloaked myself in secrecy. There was a part of me that I dared not let others see. No one must ever know that I was not the same as they.

I must admit that my secret added a touch of excitement to my life, a certain thrill that an ordinary boy could not possibly experience. I walked among those ordinary souls unnoticed, undetected. I derived a certain pleasure and sense of superiority knowing that those around me hadn't a clue as to what I was. The girls that flirted with me, the boys that admired my prowess on the soccer field, not one of them suspected what was hidden behind the facade I created for them.

My secret made me feel both powerful and vulnerable. I had no doubt I was special, even superior in a way, but I knew that danger lurked around every corner. Every friend could fast become an enemy. Every situation carried with it the potential for disaster. Being unlike all the rest carried with it a great price. I couldn't take the slightest risk of exposure. I could take no chances. Like the vampire, if I was discovered, I would be destroyed. There would be no stake driven into my heart, but my fate would be nearly as unpleasant.

The very reason I shied away from dances was why I was there, the girls. I'd avoided having a girlfriend for as long as I could. Every other boy had one, or wanted one. Every boy that had a girl paraded her around like he was toting some trophy hard won from a dangerous and highly competitive contest. Those boys that wanted a girl and did not have one were even more obvious, they practically drooled over every girl in their path. If they hadn't looked so desperate, they would probably have had a girl long ago. They were too needy. Girls didn't go for that. They were attracted to strength. They all wanted to date someone confident, bold, and brave. For all their talk of wanting someone sensitive and caring, they always went for the jocks. They acted like they wanted a sensitive guy, but the truth was those were the guys they wiped their shoes on. They weren't interested in caring boys, and desperate boys even less, they wanted jocks. They wanted guys like me.

If the truth were to be known, I was a sensitive guy, but that was one of the things I was wise enough to keep well hidden. I was openly kind and considerate, but I took pains never to let too much of that sort of thing show through. Just like I didn't let anyone know I kept a journal, or loved laying on my back and looking at the stars. It just wouldn't do to have anyone know those things about me. Everyone had to think I was nothing but an ordinary jock, and everyone did.

I didn't want a girl. They did nothing for me. No matter how beautiful they were, I found them about as sexually stimulating as a stack of steaming dog shit. Not that I had anything against them. There was nothing wrong with girls in my mind. I didn't think they were inferior or anything. They just weren't guys, it was that simple. To me, being a guy was the ultimate experience. I didn't look down on girls, but sometimes I pitied them for not being male.

I didn't want a girl, but I needed one. I knew if I didn't get one soon, all the guys would get suspicious. Already there had been questioning glances from my friends, wondering looks that silently asked what was wrong with me. I knew there was nothing wrong with me, but I knew as well that my buddies would not see it so. A guy who didn't go nuts thinking about feeling a girl up wasn't natural in my friend's way of thinking. A guy like that was some kind of freak, maybe even some kind of monster. Without doubt, there was something wrong with him. I knew my friends were wrong, but I also knew no one could ever convince them of that. That's why I could never let them know what I was.

My facade was not all that difficult to maintain. I was so unlike all the stupid homosexual stereotypes that few would even begin to guess what I was. The only things that could really expose me were my yearning glances at other young males and my lack of a girlfriend. I hid my glances as well as I could, and I was at the dance to find a girl. Not having a girlfriend made me vulnerable to suspicion. That's why I needed one, even though a girl was the last thing I wanted. I had to at least appear to want a girl, or be found out for what I was.

I knew it was not wise to gaze upon Taylor as I was doing, but at such a distance it would be difficult for any to discern what had so captured my interest. I was wise enough not to draw close, but to admire him from afar. Besides, I could not help but look at him. I felt drawn to him as I'd never felt drawn to anyone before. There was a danger, but what was life without risk?

Others found Taylor just as attractive as I. He was surrounded by half a dozen girls, all of them gazing at him with adoration in their eyes. Taylor had the look of one that was unaware of his own good looks and who was embarrassed by the attention others gave his features. The way he shyly smiled and glanced at the floor spoke of both his modesty and a certain awkwardness at being admired. Such mannerisms made him all the more attractive. Taylor absent-mindedly ran his fingers through his hair, vainly attempting to keep it back behind his ears. Even that made him more appealing. Taylor spoke little, but the girls around him hung on his every word. I found myself wishing I could hear his voice.

I was so entranced by him that I was nearly unaware of my surroundings. Everything else seemed unimportant. A voice mere inches away startled me.

"What?" I said, turning to see who it was.

"That girl over there, she's really looking you over." It was Brandon. I was so lost in my own thoughts that I hadn't even noticed him approach. I hoped he hadn't been there long.

"Huh? Oh, which one?"

"Laura, haven't you been watching her?"

"Oh, yeah. Sure I have." I lied.

I looked across the gym floor. Laura was standing just a few feet in front of Taylor. I hadn't even noticed her before, but I guessed Brandon thought I was watching her when I was really checking out Taylor. I feared I was being a little too obvious if Brandon had noticed. No harm was done however. If Brandon thought I was looking at her, so would everyone else. No one would have suspected I was drooling over a boy.

I'd talked to Laura enough times that I considered her more or less a friend. I never dreamed that she thought of me as a potential boyfriend however. I guess that such a thing was so far from my mind that I just hadn't considered it. I'd never seen it, because I wasn't looking for it. I wondered how long she'd thought of me like that.

I looked directly at Laura. She turned quickly away as my eyes met hers. That was proof enough that she was looking me over with more than casual interest.

I'd seen that look in girl's eyes before. I knew what it meant. That look frightened me.

I couldn't keep my eyes or mind on Laura however. Taylor drew my attention away from her. I couldn't help but look at him.

"Huh?" I asked when I became aware Brandon was speaking to me again.

"Are you going deaf or something?" asked Brandon. "I said 'Why don't you go over and ask her to dance?'"

"I don't know." I said, shaking my head.

"Mark, it's not like you to be so backward. Are you afraid of girls or something?"

Shit, that struck too close to home. I was afraid of them, but not for the reason Brandon suspected. The vampire feared the mirror.

My gaze drifted to Taylor yet again. In addition to the girls, a couple of guys were with him too. They looked at Taylor with the admiration that boys give other boys who are exceptionally good looking, or athletic - sort of an envious, admiring look filled with a desire to look, or be, the same. I knew that look. I caught it in the eyes of my team-mates and class-mates often enough. Don't get the idea that I'm conceited, nothing could be further from the truth. My looks were an accident of birth and my talent on the soccer field was part genetic, and part just plain, hard work. I was a better player than my team-mates, but I put a lot more work into it than any of them. I was not conceited, but I was aware of my own efforts, and good fortune. Perhaps I possessed a touch of pride in my prowess and appearance, but nothing more.

The boys near Taylor caused a touch of jealousy to rise in my chest, but I knew it was needless. Their interest in him wasn't at all the same as mine. No, I had no need to be jealous, they weren't looking for a boyfriend. Besides, I was getting way, way ahead of myself. I was interested in him, but the chances that he would feel the same about me were practically nil.

Laura was looking at me again. She was definitely interested. If only Taylor would look at me like that. Her interest frightened me, but wasn't such interest what I needed? Wasn't it the very reason I was there? Brandon standing at my side, prodding me to approach her, was a powerful reminder of what was expected of me. I was a soccer jock and I was expected to fuck, or at least date a girl and claim I fucked her. How much longer could I wait before the other boys figured out why I didn't date? If I'd been really shy, or unattractive or something, maybe I could have gotten away with not having a girl, but guys like me were expected to have a girl on their arm. It wouldn't take my buddies long to figure out why I didn't date. I'd gotten away with not dating for eighteen years, but I knew my time was running out.

Even as such thoughts flowed through my mind, my eyes were upon Taylor. I was completely taken by him. I knew it was foolish. I knew it would never come to anything. The girls surrounding him were a sign that he could never be what I wanted. I knew I had set my sights on the unobtainable, and that my failure to achieve it would crush me into dust. I couldn't help being taken however. I couldn't help but bear the slightest hope that just maybe he would feel the same as I. My heart hoped, while my mind warned me of the danger. I was a moth flying into the flame, a vampire stepping into daylight.

I feared I was kidding myself. How could he possibly be like me? Hell, I knew I'd never even have the balls to approach him. It just wasn't me. On the soccer field I was bold, fearless, sometimes reckless, but this, this was something quite different. I had long ago cloaked the real me, hidden myself from the gaze of all others because I knew they would not understand. My team-mates, my family, my friends, all of them perceived the me that I wanted them to see. To them I was the outgoing, popular, friendly, and much to be envied soccer stud. I knew that the real me was far more complicated, there were whole realms to me that few would have guessed. Even those closest to me had no idea of who I really was. That fact sometimes saddened me, but such secrecy was a necessary evil.

I was bold elsewhere, and with other things, but approaching Taylor posed far too great a risk. There was a difference between courage and stupidity. One was not a coward for stepping out of the way of a speeding truck. Taylor was quite likely that very kind of danger. He was certain destruction bearing down upon me, ready to run me over if I didn't have the sense to step out of the way.

"Mark?" said Brandon, asking with but one word why I wasn't acting on such an obvious opportunity. It was clear he could not comprehend why any boy wouldn't make a play for an attractive girl that was checking him out. I had almost forgotten again that Brandon was standing beside me. I was distracted and I knew why.

"Maybe I'll go over and talk to her later." I said. I was making up excuses for both Brandon and myself.

"Coward." said Brandon smiling.

Brandon was a good friend, but his humor cut a little too close to the truth. He had to be wondering what was wrong with me. Laura wasn't exactly hot, but she was very pretty. I was surprised some guy hadn't snatched her up. I hoped one would so she'd stop gazing at me.

"You're hopeless! Catch you later Mark." Brandon slapped me on the back and walked across the dance floor, making for a cute little blonde he'd been eyeing while he prodded me to approach Laura.

Hopeless. He had no idea. With Brandon gone, I scrutinized Taylor more thoroughly. I simply couldn't keep my eyes off him. It wasn't just that he was incredibly good looking, there was something more. I'd seen plenty of great looking guys, but none of them was like Taylor, not one of them had made me feel the way he did.

Laura was still looking at me now and then, but as I gave her no encouragement, her interest waned somewhat. I was glad and yet, I wondered if I wasn't making a mistake. I'd come to the dance to pick up a girl. Once I had a girlfriend, the guys wouldn't doubt my manhood. When it came down to it however, I just couldn't do it. It just wasn't me.

Laura looked pretty disappointed. I felt like a jerk for not at least going over and talking to her. I hated to make anyone feel bad like that, but what could I do? I didn't want to encourage her when I wasn't interested in her. Talking to her, building her hopes up, would not be an act of kindness. No, it was better that I show no interest. A little pain now would be better than more pain later. I didn't want to hurt her.

Taylor was another matter completely. He was exactly what I'd wanted all my life, well, at least for a very long time. In fact, I don't think I'd ever wanted anything quite so badly. I looked at Taylor and it was as if nothing else mattered. Once I set my eyes upon him, I felt like I'd been waiting on him, forever. I actually thought of going over to him to strike up a conversation.

No, the danger just wasn't worth it, especially considering that the boy who so took my breath away could never feel the same about me. On that path lay disappointment, pain, heartbreak, and things far worse. A deep sadness overcame me, like the loss of a near and dear friend. I was torturing myself with possibilities that had little chance of seeing the light of day.

I started to turn away, but something called me back, like a voice in my mind guiding me. Taylor's eyes met mine and something flashed between us. I can't describe it, but I felt as if, somehow, he knew my very thoughts. It was if he knew me better than I knew myself. We just looked at each other across the gym while my heart pounded in my chest.

Taylor disentangled himself from his harem and casually drew closer, seeking the same cloak of secrecy that I used to protect myself. He was far from obvious in his approach. In fact, I wasn't even sure that he was really coming to me.

If he was interested in me, as I was in him, he had to be very careful. We were, after all, surrounded by dozens upon dozens of classmates who would certainly not understand. One just does not make one's interest in another boy public, not in the homophobic world of Verona, Indiana. Taylor couldn't even be sure that I was interested in him, unless he really could read my mind. Or was my interest in him that obvious? I hoped not. Such a display was fraught with danger. Taylor moved closer, with the grace of a wolf; sleek, powerful, and silent. He nearly took my breath away.

I was terrified that Laura would see him approach me. I'd already seen Laura look over her shoulder a couple of times, trying to figure out just who or what it was that had so captured my interest. Was I getting paranoid or what? Laura wasn't even paying attention to me by any more. She was dancing. Jordan, one of the boys on my soccer team, had coaxed her out on the dance floor. I was relieved, and happy to see that someone had taken an interest in her. I felt guilty letting her just stand there when she was so obviously interested in me. That guilt disappeared once she was on the arm of another.

I didn't look directly at Taylor, but I knew exactly where he was at every moment. My heart pounded ever faster in my chest as he drew closer. Even as Taylor neared, I had my doubts. I knew was assuming far too much. Just because he was coming over to me didn't mean he was looking for a boyfriend. What was I thinking? In an instant I had altered the likelihood of a relationship with Taylor from an impossibility into a probability. I was setting myself up for a serious fall, and perhaps a dangerous one. If I'd had any sense, I would have ran.

More likely than not, he was just coming over to talk. Perhaps someone had pointed me out as a soccer jock and he was interested in trying out for the team. Perhaps he was only in search of a few pointers that would get him in. Maybe what was going through his mind wasn't at all similar to what was flowing through mine. I knew there had to be other boys like me, but so far I had found not one. Of course, it wasn't like I could just ask around. I had no idea how to seek out others like me. I couldn't even try. If I did, I might have revealed myself and all would have been lost. I lived the life of a vampire, if the villagers found out what I was, they would destroy me.

He was at my side, his smile drove all thoughts from my mind. His eyes seemed to peer into my very soul.

"I'm Taylor." His very voice made me weak in the knees. His smile took my breath away.

"Mark." I said. I wanted to say something witty, but everything I could think of was just stupid, so I didn't say anything more. I just smiled, silently saying what I could not with words. I prayed that he would not leave my side before I thought of something to say.

"You new here?" I finally asked. Wasn't I the great conversationalist?

"Yeah, we just moved from Ohio."

"Oh." More silence.

We watched the others dancing on the gym floor, a mingling mass of boys and girls pairing up. Little did they know how lucky they were to be open about what they wanted. I envied them that freedom.

"Nice dance." said Taylor.

"Yeah, but I'm not that much on dancing." It was a lie, but as close to the truth as I could come.

"Me either." he smiled again, he was always smiling.

Taylor was gorgeous. His face was so handsome it was beautiful. His arched eyebrows, finely drawn features, and sparkling green eyes captivated me. Taylor's hair was light blonde and so long it flowed down over his shoulders. He was slim, compact, firm, and no less than a dream. My heart raced standing so near him. His appearance, his voice, even his cologne intoxicated me. I felt myself drawn to him, more than that, I felt my soul drawn to him. I actually leaned toward him a little, my eyes on his lips. It was like one of those scenes in movies where a couple leans in toward each other just before they kiss. As soon as I realized what I was doing, I averted my gaze and quickly drew back.

As beautiful as I found Taylor, that beauty was the least of what attracted me. I felt as if he was the one I'd been waiting on, forever. That feeling kept coming back to me, over and over.

We kept watching the dance. We talked, about nothing in particular. Our conversation was halting, awkward. I had trouble concentrating on his words, and mine, but what we said didn't matter, so long as I could hear his voice. Little by little, the words came easier. Anyone near would have suspected nothing. We looked like all the other boys at the dance, but I knew I was in love. My body knew it too; my breath came fast, my heart raced, and other parts of my anatomy were beginning to stir. The gym felt like it was fifty degrees hotter than normal. Don't get me wrong, it wasn't just about sex, not at all. Sure, I was eighteen, and had needs, and desires, but it was my heart that responded to Taylor the most. I desired his body, but I desired his friendship, and his love, far more. I think I could have been happy forever if only I could have heard him tell me that he loved me, just once. Taylor was what I had so desperately longed for, as far back as I could recall. Once more, I felt like I had been waiting for him my entire life.

My thoughts were racing along a dozen lines at once. I knew my mind, but was Taylor on the same track? He was friendly to be sure, but that didn't necessarily lead to what I had in mind. I wanted, needed, a boyfriend, someone to love, but could he be searching for the same? Was it even possible? Wasn't that just a little much to hope, a little too good to be true? If anything, he was probably searching for a friend, and nothing more. If so, why did he pick me out? Why did he come to me all the way across the gym floor? My mind was reeling with a thousand thoughts, a thousand questions. I felt like there wasn't room for me inside my own head.

How could I be even remotely sure that Taylor was thinking along the same lines as me? More likely than not, our thoughts were far, far apart. What was running through my mind would no doubt disgust him, repel him. I knew that what seemed so beautiful to me, could be utterly repulsive to others. From where I stood, love was love, but I knew that the cruel world did not see it so. Most of those around me would not understand. What they did not understand, they feared. What they feared, they sought to destroy. I was in danger.

Taylor's friendship alone was worth pursuing, but I needed more, I had for some time. The risk was staggering however, all the more so because it could bring to an end a friendship before it had a chance to begin. I was sure we could be great friends. How could I risk such a valuable thing for something so uncertain, for a chance so slim? The danger was almost too great to even dare to think of taking the risk. I was so nervous I was practically shaking. My stomach was tying itself in knots. The thoughts running through my mind tormented me with wondrous possibilities and terrible consequences.

Taylor seemed to be looking at me with more than casual interest. There was something about the way his eyes drifted over my body now and then. Even more, there was something about the way he gazed into my eyes, as if searching, searching. I was looking at him in the same way. It was as if both of us knew what we wanted, but neither of us could bring himself to take that first step. Taylor seemed interested in me in a way no other boy had been before.

Still, I couldn't be at all sure. I wanted, needed, someone to love so bad, I feared I might be seeing what I wanted, instead of what was really there. I wanted to make contact, to discover the depths of this beautiful boy's interest, but the danger was beyond measure. What if I was wrong? What then?

The stakes were too high. Taylor could be all that I had dreamed, or he could turn and destroy me. I was lonely, but my life wasn't so bad. I had friends. I had admirers. I had soccer. I was young, and strong, and popular. I had my entire life before me. How did I dare risk all that on such a long shot?

I couldn't trust my own perceptions. I certainly wasn't thinking straight. Taylor's beautiful features and lithe, young form were distracting to the point of madness. I was in such dire need for him to be what I wanted that I could not trust my senses. I was lonely, lonely in a crowd, and I desperately needed him to be the one. It was all too much. A terror fell upon me that frightened me to my very soul. I felt sick. I panicked.

"I've got to go." I stammered.

I didn't even wait for a response. I actually turned and bolted from the gym. I could feel Taylor's eyes on me. I'm sure he wondered what the hell was going on. I wondered the same, I'd never run from anything like that before. I felt like a coward and still, I ran.

I ran out of the gym, through the parking lot, and across the soccer fields. It was night, but the bright light of the moon almost made it seem like day. I kept running, beyond the practice field I knew so well, straight on into the woods. I ran along the paths used by lovers, and the cross country team. I ran past the trees. I ran until my breath came in gasps and my heart threatened to explode in my chest and still, I ran on. I ran from my fears. I ran until I couldn't run any more. I collapsed upon a small hillock in the middle of a clearing. I lay on my back panting, drawing great mouthfuls of oxygen into my lungs.

As my heart and breath gradually slowed, I stared up at the stars, so big and bright I felt like I could reach out and touch them. That was me, always reaching for the stars, always reaching for dreams that couldn't come true. A single tear rolled down my cheek, a tear of loneliness and isolation. Having what I wanted most in all the world dangled in front of me, increased a hundred fold the pain that was always with me. Taylor was my dream come true, or at least he seemed to be. But how could I be sure? How could I take such a chance?

At my school, anyone suspected of being gay was treated mercilessly. I remembered only too well a boy named Ronnie from my freshman year. Ronnie was a really nice boy, but thin and pale and his voice had a really high pitch. He was cute, but kind of looked like a girl. Some of the guys slapped a "queer" label on him and made his life a living hell. He couldn't go anywhere without someone calling him names or making fun of him. All the guys called him "prissy" and "cock-sucker", right to his face. Well, not all the guys, I never did. I'd never treat anyone like that. I never knew if Ronnie was even gay. He had a high voice and looked kind of feminine, but I knew better than anyone how stupid all the stereotypes were. I was gay and I was nothing like that. The way he talked and the way he looked had no more to do with whether or not he was gay than what he liked on his pizza.

I guess it didn't matter if he was really gay or not. All the guys just assumed he was and treated him like a piece of shit. I couldn't believe that anyone would treat another human being like that. Somehow Ronnie toughed it out and finished the school year. I hadn't seen him since then. I guess his family moved or something. I didn't blame him for not coming back.

I wanted to be with Taylor more than anything, but what would happen if something went wrong? What if he wasn't interested in me? What if he just called me a fag and told everyone what I'd said to him? I'd be just like Ronnie. I couldn't face that.

Our whole community was down on homosexuals. The year before, at the same time everyone was ragging on Ronnie, my social studies teacher put up this poster that had pictures of Michelangelo, Errol Flynn, Walt Whitman, and other historical figures. At the bottom was a message that read, "Sexual orientation does not determine a person's ability to make a mark, let alone make history." I always liked that poster. It made me feel good about myself. I had a pretty good self image anyway, but knowing that guys like Michelangelo were gay made me feel like I was in pretty good company. I was no art buff, and his paintings weren't my kind of thing, but that dude kicked ass when he painted! A lot of famous people were gay, most people just didn't know about it.

Anyway, this bitch named Campbell started throwing a fit about that poster when her son Ryan, who was in my class, told her about it. She raised a big stink to get it removed. She even had the gall to say that her problem with the poster had nothing to do with homosexuals, she just didn't think it had any educational value. Bull shit! If that poster hadn't of been about gays, she wouldn't have given a damn. There was a poster right next to it with a little cute little puppy on it that said, "Have a nice day." Where was the educational value of that? Why didn't old Campbell get all shitty about that poster?

I went to the school board meeting just to see what everyone said about it. A bunch of people were all upset about it. More than one called it "immoral". One even said, "God made Adam and Eve, not Adam and Steve." Hearing that made me sick. It was unbelievable how nasty most of the people there were about it. Mr. Hahn, my social studies teacher, tried to defend what he was doing, but those bastards just ignored him. It was clear they'd showed up with their minds already made up about the whole thing.

Campbell, forgetting her earlier comment, complained that the poster promoted the homosexual lifestyle. Now how in the hell did it do that? Everyone seemed to think that being gay was like some kind of club that you could join. They acted like gays were out trying to recruit new members or something. What a stack of shit! I knew better than any of them that sexual orientation was no more a matter of choice than eye color, or height. I guess they all thought the poster was saying that if you wanted to paint like Michelangelo, you had to turn gay!

The local newspaper did a story on the whole thing, which I have to admit was pretty objective. Whoever wrote that article was about the only one that was objective however. Even some big national society got involved and denounced the poster. A civil liberties group stepped in on Mr. Hahn's side. What a big deal over a poster.

I think what struck me the most was the local pastors and church people that spoke out against the poster, and homosexuality. Mind you, not all of them did, I don't want to stereotype church people as a bad lot, because a lot of them are really good, but those that were down on gays made me sick. I couldn't believe some of the stuff they said. They made it sound like all gays were just perverts and child molesters. One of them actually referred to homosexuals as "the sons of satan". The worst was when one of the local preachers actually said "God hates gays." I simply couldn't believe it.

They acted like homosexuals were some kind of freaks. All that really pissed me off. I was gay and I was none of the things they were saying. I wondered about the rules people who attend church were supposed to follow. What happened to doing unto others as you would have them do unto you? What happened to judge not that ye be not judged? What happened to love thy neighbor and all that? As far as I was concerned, those who said such awful things about homosexuals weren't Christians at all. In my eyes they had abandoned their mission and betrayed the very ideas they spouted so readily. They were no less than hypocrites. I had to remind myself that not all church people were like that. It's just too bad some of them used religion for their own personal agenda. Personally, I wouldn't have been eager to explain my actions to God if I was them.

In the end, Mr. Hahn just took all of his posters down. I know he felt kind of bad about it, but everyone was ragging on him about it all the time. There was such a fuss he couldn't even teach. His students were what was important to him, so he took the posters down so he could teach us. I guess taking all of them down was his way of protesting.

I was really getting off the topic, but my mind raced from one thing to another sometimes and that whole incident, and the way all the guys treated Ronnie, really got to me. Those incidents taught me one lesson well; Verona, Indiana was no place for homosexuals. Everyone I knew acted like all gays should be driven into the center of town and stoned.

With all that to fear, how could I possibly take a chance on Taylor? If he wasn't the boy I thought he was, and narked me out, I was finished. I'd be just like Ronnie, only worse. Everyone wouldn't just guess I was gay, they would know. I wasn't in the least ashamed of what I was. I saw no reason at all to be ashamed. But that wouldn't stop my class-mates from making my life a living hell. I couldn't stand up to everyone!

I knew how illogical it was to even consider opening up to Taylor, but my heart, and my soul, cried out for him. What if he really was the one I'd been waiting on all my life? What if he really felt the same way about me as I felt about him? How could I pass up what might be my only shot at true happiness, true love?

I did love him. I know it might sound silly to love someone I'd just met, but I loved him with all my heart. I didn't feel like we were strangers at all. I felt as if I'd known him for lifetimes.

I watched the stars overhead, wondering if Taylor could see them too. I wondered what he'd thought when I ran out of the gym. He probably thought I was some kind of freak. I wondered where he was now. Was he dancing with some girl, or was he just standing there watching, wondering where I was? My heart ached for him.

I closed my eyes. My heart was still pounding in my chest from the miles I'd run. I felt like I'd been thinking and watching the stars for hours, but it had been just a few minutes. My breath still came in gasps and I was actually shaking. My stomach felt tight, and ached. I was on the verge of breaking into tears. I was confused, and tormented.

The possibilities that arose with Taylor highlighted the inadequacies of my life. I had much, but I lacked even more. The loneliness, the utter isolation, the enveloping sadness, all this, and more, was brought to the surface to torment me for being different. How many times had I looked into the eyes of another boy, hoping to find someone like me, someone who could end my isolation? How many times had I been disappointed? How many times had I realized that my hopes were futile, yet again?

I didn't even have the solace of a friend to help me through my troubles. Yes, I had friends, but not one that I could open up to, not one that I felt would understand. I did not dare speak my mind with any of them. No one would have understood, no one could. Such was the life of a vampire. I was alone with my pain, utterly, irrevocably alone. I was miserable.

I opened my eyes. The stars were still there. It was good to know that there was something steady in my life, something to hold onto. No matter what happened down here, the stars would always be there. I arose and walked back the way I had come, my mind filled with possibilities and dangers. It didn't seem to matter how long I thought, I never got any closer to an answer.

2 A Brave New World

I didn't see Taylor the next day at school, and you can be sure I was looking for him. His first day was to be the following Monday, but I didn't know it then and kept watching for him everywhere I went. I hadn't been able to get him out of my mind for a moment since the night before. I even dreamed about him, even though I couldn't remember what the dream was about. I could almost remember, it was right there before me, but I couldn't quite grasp it.

I was distracted all day. I was half through algebra class before I realized I was writing the name Taylor over and over in my notebook. I closed the cover quickly, thankful no one had noticed it. I had to be careful. I couldn't afford to slip up like that.

I was glad when time for soccer practice came around. I could lose myself in strenuous physical activity and clear my mind of the debate that was constantly raging within. I hadn't stopped thinking for a moment about Taylor, or if I should take the chance and tell him how I felt.

Coach McFadden had us running around the soccer field until we were ready to drop. The pain in my legs and chest helped me to clear my thoughts. I concentrated on the drills and worked hard on my passing and ball handling skills. I always took soccer serious, but that day I worked extra hard at focusing on the task at hand. Thinking about Taylor made me happy, and yet it terrified me, and made me sad, even depressed. I didn't know how to deal with all the emotions that were roiling within me, so I fought to ignore them. Soccer practice allowed me to do that, at least for a while.

As soon as practice ended, Taylor was right back in my mind. Actually, he'd never left it for a moment. It was just that I'd been able to put my debate aside. I could always see him in my mind. I could tell I had it bad for Taylor. I didn't even pay any attention to the guys that surrounded me in the locker room, or the showers. My eyes usually wandered when I was around all those naked and semi-naked guys. That was one of the cool things about being gay. Any of my friends who have killed to have been able to look around in the girl's locker room and showers like that! As far as I was concerned, those guys weren't even there. Nothing mattered but Taylor.

Saturday afternoon we had a soccer game on our home field. Our team had been a little weak since Brad, our other center forward, had left. Devon, who temporarily filled the vacancy, just couldn't cut it and I was pretty much left to handle center forward by myself. We were still undefeated however.

I scored a goal less than five minutes into the first quarter. Our opponents were lousy at defense. It was almost like they weren't even there. I nearly felt sorry for them as I dodged and parried, cutting through them with such ease it made them look foolish. By the end of the first half we were beating them by 8-0. It was pretty sad.

During the second half, I started taking more chances with the ball. I made passes I wouldn't have in a close game. I passed the ball to guys that normally didn't take a shot. Some of them even scored. Coach didn't like it much, but the rest of us had fun. I knew coach was kind of pissed at me for not playing harder, but why run up the score? Why not give some of the other guys a chance? I think I had a much greater grasp of the concepts of "sportsmanship" and "team" than coach did. If it was up to him, he'd have ran up the score as much as possible. I knew he was pissed during the game. I also knew he'd forget all about it as soon as we won.

I glanced up into the stands just as I passed the ball. I froze for a moment. Taylor was there and he was watching me. I actually forgot I was in a soccer game for a few seconds. That had never happened to me before. I just stood there and looked at him. He saw me gawking at him and smiled. My heart melted.

"Mark! Get in the game!" yelled coach.

I came to my senses. The ball was half way down the field. I raced to catch up, even though Devon was cutting right through our opponents defense. He scored before I got there. Devon was elated and I was happy for him, he didn't get to score all that often.

For the rest of the game I was distracted. I kept checking to see if Taylor was watching me. Whenever I looked up, his eyes were upon me. I felt that he wasn't just there to watch the game, he was there to watch me. It made me feel all happy and warm inside. Then I wondered if he was really there on account of me. Might I not being seeing it that way because that's how I wanted it to be? I just didn't know.

The whistle blew three times and the game was over. We won 14-0. Taylor was cheering at the top of his lungs. I ran off the field with my team-mates. I showered fast, but by the time I came back out, Taylor was gone.

I was antsy the rest of the weekend. I tried to keep myself busy, but my mind was always drifting back to Taylor. What was I going to do about him? I knew what I wanted to do. I knew what I should do. Unfortunately, those two things were exact opposites. I wanted to tell Taylor how I felt, but I knew I should just forget him. That was a laugh, I hadn't been able to get him out of my mind for a moment since we'd met. I felt all nervous and I couldn't eat, I couldn't sleep. Forget about him, that was impossible!

On Sunday afternoon Brandon called me up and asked me to go to Koontz Lake with him. The lake was not far out of town and was the hang out place for all the high school kids. I needed something to do, so I accepted. It was likely to be one of the last good days for going to the lake anyway. Soon it would be too cold.

The sun was nice and warm when we arrived and I pulled off my shirt and tossed it in the car. Brandon did the same. Brandon had a really nice build. He was extremely attractive. It was odd, but I wasn't sexually attracted to him. We were pretty good friends, kind of like brothers in a way. I'd always thought of him like that and hadn't fantasized about him like I had so many of the other guys. Well, maybe I had a few thoughts along those lines, but not many.

The beach was filled with high school kids, including a lot of guys from my team. I knew just about everyone there. It was like one big party with loud music and everyone swimming or tanning. I swam for a while, then lay sunning on the beach. The warm sun felt good on my naked skin. I'd spent a lot of time in the sun all summer and was tanned a nice golden brown. I just lay there with my eyes closed for a long time, enjoying the sun on my chest, the voices of my friends, and the music.

Suddenly, my eyes popped open. It was him. I recognized his voice. I sat up and turned. There was Taylor talking to some of the guys. He was wearing bright blue swim trunks and nothing else. He was gorgeous! His voice was musical, so happy and filled with life. He was smiling. That's one thing I loved about Taylor. He was always smiling.

He looked in my direction and our eyes locked. I looked away. I didn't know what to do. I was panic stricken. I felt stupid for being so afraid. I was acting like a giddy pre-pubescent girl and that I was not! I got up, brushed off the sand, and walked over to Taylor.

I talked to him, and the guys. While we were speaking with the others, our eyes kept meeting. It was clear there was something between us. I just didn't know what. All the old questions, hopes, and doubts flooded my mind. I was drowning in a sea of uncertainty. I was lost in a universe with delights beyond imagining and terrors to freeze the soul.

I had to get away, just for a while. I had to think. I drifted away from Taylor and my friends and walked along the beach to the little bath house where swimmer's could shower and change. I went inside. No one was there.

I was so nervous I was trembling. I knew what I wanted, but was afraid. I was no coward, I had reason to fear, but still... I closed my eyes tightly, shutting out the entire world. I was so confused I didn't know what to think. I was terrified of what could happen, but I loved Taylor so much it hurt. What if he was the one I'd been waiting on all my life? My mind traveled down the paths I'd trod before, going over the possibilities and the dangers yet again, coming no closer to a solution than ever. I was so upset I was almost in tears.

I'd decided to take a chance on Taylor a hundred times, and I'd decided not to dare the risk just as many times. I felt like the jack-ass in doubt who stood between two hay-stacks and starved to death. I had to make a decision or go out of my mind!

I heard footfalls, someone was coming. I opened my eyes and fought to rein in my emotions. What I could not share, I had to hide. I'd grown rather adept at hiding my feelings from others. I fought to pull myself together. I had only seconds. The façade had to go back up.

The footsteps drew nearer, rounded the corner. It was Taylor. He'd followed me. He looked at me for a moment before he spoke.

"Why did you run away Mark? At the dance? I thought we were becoming friends." He spoke with an earnestness that made me feel we'd already been friends forever. Why did I feel as if I already knew him? His bright eyes peered at me. I felt as he could look into my very soul.

"I'm sorry." I said. "I…, I…" I actually could not speak. I could not tell him what was running through my mind. The stakes were just too great. I was in hell. Before me was a boy for whom I felt great love, and I could not begin to tell him of it for fear. For fear of rejection? Yes, but for far greater fears as well; the fear of being exposed, the fear of others knowing that I was different, that I dreamed of other boys at night instead of girls. All I wanted was someone to love and someone to love me back, but because I was different, I couldn't even try for that love the way others could. Once again I envied all my classmates. How wonderful it must be for them to be so open and free!

Taylor was looking at me with infinite patience, and, understanding? I had nearly forgotten he was there, so lost in my own thoughts had I become. It was almost funny. I hadn't been able to get him out of my head for days, and now that he was standing in front of me, I almost forgot he was there.

Taylor could clearly tell I was distraught. His eyes were filled with compassion. I felt safe in that gaze in a way that I'd never felt safe before. I closed my eyes and swallowed hard. When I opened them, Taylor was still peering at me, standing there as if he'd wait forever. He didn't push me, didn't prod me, he just, waited. A meek, but genuine smile played across my lips. I looked into his eyes.

"I ran because I was afraid." I admitted. No one would ever know how hard it was to speak those words. I could have more easily jumped from a plane, without a parachute.

"Afraid." he said quietly, as if turning the concept over in his mind, fitting the piece into a puzzle he was carefully putting together.

I was trembling, despite my best efforts to prevent it. I had to escape the private hell I lived in, and yet the mere attempt was harder than anything I'd ever done before. I summoned all my courage. I had to make the attempt. Mine was not a life to live. Maybe Taylor would slug me in the face. Maybe he'd spit on me and tell me what a freak I was. Maybe he'd tell everyone about me. It didn't matter anymore. I had to try. I owed myself a chance at happiness, even if the risk was beyond measure.

I was not a coward, far, far from it. I had taken many risks in my life. My parents and even friends had jumped me more than once for placing my body in jeopardy, but what was life if one did not live it? This was but another risk, but so much more, for it was not my body that was in danger, it was the very essence of what was me. I had made up my mind. I would not run from this danger a second time. I was no coward. What I was about to do required courage almost beyond belief. There would be no more debating, no more hesitating. I would make my stand. I would either prevail, or be destroyed.

"I like you." I hesitated. "A lot." I paused yet again. I had never been so awkward, nor so inept with my words. I knew the words I wanted to speak and yet it took a supreme effort to force them from my lips. I wanted to be eloquent, impressive, instead I was a bumbling fool. Finally, I just blurted it out. "I love you Taylor."

There, I had said it. It was out and I couldn't take it back. No matter what happened, there was no way to undo what I'd done. I felt like I'd just condemned myself to a long and painful death. I looked into Taylor's eyes, knowing that the fear in my own was plain to see. Taylor held my life in his hands. I'd literally given him the power to destroy me if he chose. I was a vampire who had placed a wooden stake in his hand. I waited to see if he would thrust it into my heart.

Taylor looked at me. I could not read him. He stepped toward me and I had to fight to keep from flinching. I really expected him to punch me. I really expected him to knock my teeth out. I looked deeper into his eyes and read understanding there, but yet I was still afraid. I couldn't hope that he would really understand. I couldn't let myself have that hope, for fear it would prove false. Taylor wrapped his arms around me and hugged me tight.

"I would never have had the balls to say that." said Taylor. He leaned back and peered into my eyes, his hands on my shoulders. "But, I'm glad you did."

I looked into his eyes. What I read there filled my heart with joy and forced all sad and painful thoughts from my mind.

"I know it seems impossible so fast, but I love you too Mark. I can't explain it. I don't know why. I just know that I do." I understood him perfectly.

He hugged me close once more. I held him tight, practically crushing him in my arms. I never wanted to let him go. I don't think I had ever been as happy as I was at that moment. At last, I had someone to love, and someone to love me. The fears fled from my mind and left only the possibilities, only the potential joys. The entire universe shifted. My whole life changed.

We stood there, holding each other close, for as long as we dared. We were in a public place, our class-mates mingling just outside, and the likelihood of being discovered together increased with each moment that passed. Still, we held one another tight. Our long search was over, at last, we'd found each other.

We exchanged phone numbers, hugged yet again, then Taylor departed, returning to the beach. I followed a few minutes later, I saw him once again talking with friends. I swam for a few minutes, then joined them, my eyes meeting Taylor's over and over again as we talked. There was so much I wanted to say to him, but it would all have to wait. We were surrounded by others and could not speak freely in the least.

I was bursting with joy as I walked the short distance from Brandon's car to my house. I felt like I could walk on air. My mom greeted me as I walked in the door.

"Mark, what happened to you?"

"Huh?"

"You just look… happy."

I smiled. I guess my mood was quite obvious. I mean, I had barely walked in the door and mom read me like a book.

"Yes!" I said. "I am!" I leaned down and gave her a great hug. My mother is rather small, only about five foot six and thin. At eighteen, I was already six feet tall and weighed 165 pounds. Whenever I hugged her, she seemed to get lost in my arms.

"What happened?"

"Just a good day." I yelled over my shoulder, heading for my room. I felt a pang of sadness that I couldn't share with her the real reason for my happiness. There was just no way she could understand. Besides, I wasn't about to tell my parents about my sexual preferences - not mom and sure as hell not dad. He would absolutely freak! My dad thought I was some kind of soccer playing stud jock, which I was, but I knew he'd go nuts if he found out I was into guys. The very thought of telling him filled me with terror. No, I would never go there.

Actually, I wouldn't have talked about what had happened with my parents even if I had fallen for a girl. We just never talked about stuff like that. Neither of my parents had ever breathed a word to me about sex. I was sure they'd both faint dead away if I said "penis" or "condom" or any such word in their presence.

Sex was just something we never discussed. It was like the topic didn't even exist. Anything vaguely related to sex embarrassed the hell out of my parents. If we were all watching television, my dad would get all uncomfortable if there was a bra commercial or something like that. He'd grab up a paper and start looking at it. If any douche commercials came on he was right out of that room fast.

Mom was about the same. If a couple started making out on the screen, she'd suddenly remember something she had to do in the kitchen. I'm sure they'd both bolt from the room if I started talking about sex. There was no fucking way I'd ever tell them I was in love with a boy!

The momentary sadness left me quickly. Nothing could spoil my day. I had a boyfriend at last. And what a boyfriend! Taylor was cute beyond my wildest dreams. I loved everything about him: his hair, his face, his voice, his body, the way he smiled, the way he talked, just - everything!

I lay back on my bed and thought about him. I couldn't get him out of my mind and I had absolutely no desire to do so. I had been so alone and then, bang, Taylor was in my life. I had wanted someone like him for so long, and suddenly there he was.

I looked around my room at my stereo, my computer, my CD collection, and my sports trophies. I couldn't wait to show Taylor all my stuff. I was particularly proud of my trophies. I had played soccer for as long as I could remember and my teams had won many championships. I'd been named most valuable player more than once too. I loved soccer and it was something I was good at. I couldn't wait to share that with Taylor. I wondered if he played. I wondered a lot of things. I was in a daze the rest of the night. I couldn't sleep well. My mind raced, all with thoughts of Taylor. My whole world shifted, I saw it all in relation to him. How had I survived all those years before I'd met him? It seemed almost impossible. I could not imagine life without Taylor.

3 Soccer Boy

I was in a dream world. I was so happy, I'd felt like I could fly. My whole world had opened up. My future had seemed so bleak, at least as far as having a boyfriend was concerned, but suddenly my life seemed almost too good to be true. The truth is, things were so good, it frightened me a little. I was more than half afraid that it really was a dream. Maybe I'd fallen asleep on the hill by the school while I was looking at the stars. Or worse, maybe the whole thing was a dream. Maybe there was no Taylor at all. No, he was real. It was all real.

My car was in the shop, so I walked to school on Monday morning. I didn't mind walking at all. The weather was fine and hot. It was a gorgeous September day. The whole world seemed beautiful to me. I looked upon everything around me with a new set of eyes. I couldn't believe what had happened. I actually had a boyfriend. I loved him, and best of all, he loved me! He was so cute too, and so hot. I got a warm, fuzzy feeling just thinking about him. Taylor was my blonde babe. No, that didn't sound right, it was too girlish, and there was nothing girlish about Taylor. I thought about him all the time, and not just about having sex with him, I thought mostly about just being with him.

As I neared school reality began to set in. I wanted to share my happiness with the whole world, but the world would not approve. I had almost forgotten I was a vampire. I could just imagine what my classmates would have thought if they knew I was in love with another boy. I was popular at school. I had a reputation for being tough, but yet nice, and funny too. Mainly, I was known as a jock. I had participated in football, swimming, and even a little track. Soccer was my real love however and at that I excelled. I knew that it was my prowess at soccer that really made me popular. I was a jock and jocks ruled! What would they all think if they knew I was gay?

I doubt few of them even suspected. It's not that my classmates were stupid, but they all seemed to buy the old stereotypes. Gay guys were effeminate, girl-like. They were pansies, they spoke with a lisp, and had weak wrists. They wanted to be girls. They were wimps afraid of being men. They were freaks of nature. I knew the stereotypes were a bunch of crap. Sure, there were gay guys that fit the bill. I bet there were straight guys who'd have fit it just as well. The truth was that any stereotype was just plain wrong. There were all types of gay guys, just as there were all types of guys. It's too bad more people couldn't understand that.

I certainly didn't fit the stereotype. I was a known jock, not exactly the pansy type. I didn't have a lisp and I wanted to be a girl about as much as I wanted my dick ripped off. I loved being a guy. I enjoyed it. It rocked! Everything about being male was cool. No, no one would suspect me of being gay, unless I tipped my hand. I felt my old ways returning. I was the vampire who lived in secrecy to avoid destruction. I was both powerful and vulnerable. If the villagers found me out, I'd get a stake through the heart for sure. Things were even more complicated than they had been before, I had another vampire to protect.

I wondered what to do about my relationship with Taylor. I wished we could hold hands the way other couples did in school. I wished we could kiss in the cafeteria and have all the other guys clap and howl. I wished we could make our feelings for each other public, or at least not have to hide them, but I knew that could not be. That knowledge took some of the joy from my heart, but I wasn't going to let it get me down. I didn't care if anyone else approved. I didn't care what they might think. I'd never cared if anyone else approved of my clothes, my hair, my music, or anything else and I didn't give a damn about whether or not they'd approve of me and Taylor. Their feelings on the subject were irrelevant. Taylor was all that mattered.

Being gay was becoming more accepted. There were places where gay guys could be open about their relationships. There were places where they could walk holding hands, and even kiss in public. There were places where no one gave it a second thought. There were places where prejudice didn't exist. Verona, Indiana was not one of those places. Like most of the Midwest, it was stuck fast in the dark ages. Even more so than most places. Yeah, I could be open about what I was in Verona, about four hundred years after I was dead.

One of the first people I met in the halls was Taylor. We exchanged a high five. It was a very jock thing to do. I can't explain it, doing that sort of thing just came natural. I'd rather have had a hug, that would have come natural too, but it was out of the question. Besides, our eyes said it all. Taylor lit up when he saw me and I know my eyes sparkled with happiness. In a way our secret relationship added spice to my life and I'm sure it did to his as well. There we were surrounded by our class-mates, and not one of them suspected that Taylor was my boyfriend.

"Mark, can you tell me where Mr. Geoffrey's first period English class is?"

"Cool, you have him first period? So do I, come on."

I led Taylor through the halls. It was his first day at my school. He was at the dance on Thursday and the lake on the weekend only because his neighbor (one of the girls I saw admiring him) invited him along to meet a few people. Boy did I owe her big!

I'd never been so happy to go to class. Now that Taylor would be there I thought I might even start to like English. Yeah right! I did like writing a lot, but I didn't give a damn about English class. I mean, who's ever going to diagram a sentence in real life? I don't see why it matters that I know all about verbs, adjectives, pronouns, and all that other crap. I know how to use the words. I can speak and write quite well without knowing any of that. Notice that I said "speak and write well", not "speak and write good". See what I mean. I don't need that shit!

Anyway, English class was another chance to spend time with Taylor, so at last it had a purpose. Time with Taylor was something I really wanted. So far, we hadn't even really talked. It was funny. I already considered him my boyfriend, but we barely knew each other. I was rushing into everything way too fast, but I couldn't help myself. I wasn't taking a risk where Taylor was concerned however. I knew in my heart that we were meant to be together. I read it in his eyes when we were alone together in the bath house out at Koontz Lake. I could just feel it. I was never wrong about stuff like that. I'd had my doubts while gazing at him across the gym floor at the dance, but after we held each other close, there were no more doubts in my mind.

Taylor sat next to me in English. I leaned over and talked with him before class started.

"Taylor, are you busy after school? Maybe we can do something together?"

"I'd like that, but I'm going to see if I can get on the soccer team. Can we do something after that?"

My whole face lit up. Oh yes!

"You play soccer?"

"I love it!" said Taylor. "I've played since I was a little kid."

Taylor was even into soccer! Things could not get any better!

Mr. Geoffrey started class before I had a chance to talk to Taylor about the soccer team, but I was hyped with the idea of him joining. I was so happy, even Mr. Geoffrey's monotone lecture on the proper use of prepositions didn't bring me down. I had trouble sitting still. I fidgeted the entire period and couldn't keep from tapping my fingers on my desk. Mr. Geoffrey glared at me for that, but I just couldn't help it. I was so pumped up someone was going to have to shoot me with a tranquilizer gun to calm me down. I felt like that a lot on the soccer field, but it was a first in English class.

Every time I met Taylor that day, I wanted to touch him. I could barely keep my hands off him. I did put my hand on his shoulder a few times, and touched his forearm once. I even draped my arm across his shoulder for a few moments before I sat down beside him at lunch, but that drew some looks from the other guys, so I pulled my arm away pretty fast. I had to really watch myself. I couldn't just do what came naturally. I had to remain on my toes. I felt like I was a Jewish boy trying to escape notice in Nazi Germany or a vampire avoiding sunlight and mirrors. I had to maintain my cloak of secrecy, or be destroyed. Discretion was more important than ever. It wasn't just me anymore, I had Taylor to protect as well.

I had hoped for a chance to really talk to Taylor at lunch, but we were quickly joined by some of my buddies and a small flock of girls. Being popular has it's disadvantages. The flock of girls were always somewhat of a problem with me. I knew some of them were after me. They flirted with me like crazy sometimes. But, of course, I wasn't interested. Not that I didn't like them, I enjoyed their company, but I sure didn't want to date them.

I had been more than a little worried that others might think I was queer because I wasn't dating. I mean, I had plenty of opportunities. I was good looking, athletic, popular, and girls were obviously after me. Why wouldn't a guy like that date unless he was gay? I looked at Taylor. My relationship with him was going to be a problem. We'd be spending a great deal of time together and rumors were sure to spread. It was bad enough with just me, but once Taylor and I started hanging out together, the problem would increase ten fold. We were going to have to do something about that, I just wasn't sure what yet.

Taylor was drawing plenty of attention himself. The guys liked him. There seemed to be a natural connection between athletic guys. I can't really explain it. I guess we just had sports as a common interest and that brought us all together. Taylor wasn't as much of the jock type as I was. He was athletic and all that, but he had more of a sensitive nature and it showed. Where anyone who looked at me would immediately think "soccer player", they might look at Taylor and think "artist" or "poet", just as fast as they would "baseball player" or something like that. Of course, that's one of the things that attracted me to him. Taylor had a sensitive side that I found appealing. He was a jock with the soul of a poet.

The girls were certainly flirting up a storm with him. Who could blame them? Taylor was downright cute with his angelic face and gorgeous blonde hair. His firm, well formed body didn't hurt matters either. Andrea, a cute little brunette who'd been after me since the sixth grade was really giving him the eye. I watched her as I ate. Her eyes were lit up with the same admiration that I knew showed in my own. I yearned to call to her, "Too bad Andrea, he's mine!"

Taylor was good natured with everyone. He joked around with the guys and he flirted with the girls. He seemed to know how to flirt with the females just enough to deflect suspicion, without getting their hopes up. It gave me a warm feeling to see that he cared enough to spare the feelings of the girls. I mean, as cute as he was, he could have teased them mercilessly. I knew heterosexual guys who did that. They knew some of the less attractive girls had it for them bad. They flirted with them, pretended to be interested in them, built their hopes up, then dumped on them. They thought it was funny. I thought it was cruel. Taylor would never do that to anyone. I could just tell. Taylor wasn't that kind of guy. He'd flirt, but never take things too far. He'd never intentionally hurt anyone.

Taylor paid plenty of attention to me too. We couldn't speak freely surrounded by others, but there was still plenty we could talk about. I learned he was a natural at soccer and that got my hopes up. There was only one spot open on the team, recently vacated by Brad, whose family had moved to Texas. A few guys had already tried for it, but coach shot them down, one by one. It wasn't easy making the varsity soccer team. I hoped Taylor could do it, and I thought he had a good chance. The open position was center forward, exactly what Taylor had played at his last school. Even better, center forward was also my position. If Taylor got on the team, we'd be practicing and playing side by side.

Taylor tried for the team that afternoon during practice. He nailed it! The coach was so impressed with him he gave him the spot immediately. Coach

McFadden was one of those "win or don't come back" types and he practically drooled over Taylor's ball handling abilities. I know coach was thinking "championship" as he slapped Taylor on the butt and sent him to the locker room to change. We were a tough team, but a bit weak on offense since Brad left. I was an awesome forward (if I do say so myself), but I couldn't do it all alone and the guys who had filled in since Brad departed just didn't cut it. My friend Devon had been filling in most of the time and the relief on his face was evident when coach announced he was moving him back to right half-back. Devon was sharp, but just not up to the pressure in the center. Everyone was happy; coach, Devon, Taylor, the team, and most of all, me!

Taylor looked awesome as he ran onto the field in his blue and white soccer uniform, his golden hair flowing behind him. He was so beautiful it made my heart ache. I know, I shouldn't have been so hung up on someone because of their looks. That was pretty shallow. It was okay in this case however, because I was hung up on Taylor in every way. His looks were just part of that. If, God forbid, he was in a terrible accident that messed up his looks, I knew I'd still love him. I knew it wouldn't change the way I felt about him. No, I wasn't shallow. I just appreciated what I had.

Coach divided up the team and we played a practice game. Taylor and I worked together like a well oiled machine. It was like we could read each others mind. We always knew just where, and when, to pass. We cut through our opponents like a hot knife through butter. We just couldn't be stopped. It wasn't long before the team was chanting "Taylor! Taylor!" Taylor was in, he was one of us.

Perhaps I should have felt a little jealous, maybe even a little insecure that there was another hot shot on the team. I generally defended my position aggressively. I let no one stand in my way. Nothing was further from my mind on that day however. I was more thrilled with Taylor's success than I was my own. I loved him.

Coach McFadden held Taylor back a few minutes after practice, so I showered, dressed and waited for him in the gym. He came out of the locker room looking so attractive in his jeans and polo shirt. The open buttons revealed just a hint of his hard, tanned chest and made my heart beat just a little faster. I peered deeply into his blue-green eyes. He smiled, it made him all the more breath-taking. I still couldn't believe this blonde stud-puppy was my boyfriend.

"Taylor, can you come to my house?"

"Sure," he said, "Hey Mark, call me Tay, all my close friends back in Ohio called me that."

"Sure Tay." I liked the sound of that.

We walked toward my house, in no particular hurry. We had so much to discuss, a lifetime of catching up to do. There was so much I didn't know about Tay, and he knew equally little about me. The more we talked, the more we had in common. So many of our interests were the same, it was like Tay had been specially designed, just for me.

We'd known each other such a short time, and yet, I felt like I'd known Tay forever. Maybe that stuff about reincarnation was true. Maybe we'd spent whole life-times together. I didn't know about that, but I liked the idea of spending life-times with Tay.

I was right about him being a poet. He did write poetry. When I read some, days later, it was like his poems let me peer directly into his soul. I'd never been that big on poetry. To be honest, I'd always hated the stuff and sure couldn't write it myself. Taylor's poems were different however. They weren't about trees or flowers or some shit like that, they were about how he felt. I guess I connected with them because they were so much like what I'd felt. I could feel the loneliness in his poems. I could feel the heartache, the pain, the desperate longing, the sense of waiting for someone, the fear of being exposed. I'd never have been able to get all those things down on paper, but Taylor could. He was a poet.

Taylor was far more sensitive that I was. I don't mean that I didn't care for anyone, or about anyone, or any of that. It's just that I didn't think all that much about it. My thoughts were always wrapped around the next soccer game, playing basketball with my friends, or buying some new CD. I don't know. I guess I was just a physical kind of guy. I had feelings. I just didn't dwell on them. Taylor did. He was so sweet and thoughtful. That attracted me to him all the more. In a lot of ways he was just like me, but in others he was vastly different, almost my opposite. Maybe it was true, maybe opposites did attract. Of course, our similarities were pretty attractive to me too. I mean, a boyfriend who was a kick-ass soccer player, how could anyone beat that?

"You impressed the hell out of the coach." I said.

"I guess so, I'm just glad I got on the team. I'd die if I wasn't able to play soccer!"

"Are you sure you aren't me?" I asked. "Soccer is my life. Or at least it was, now there's something far more important to me."

I smiled at Tay and he grinned from ear to ear.

"You're so cute." I couldn't help saying it. Taylor actually blushed. He possessed the shyness of a little boy, and the beauty of a young man.

"Stop!" said Tay. "You're embarrassing me."

"Okay, but it's true."

"Thanks," he said. "And since you brought it up, I could say the same about you." It was my turn to get embarrassed. I had never learned to take a compliment.

"We're getting pretty sappy." I said.

"Hey, you're the one who started it." said Tay. He was right, but how could I help it? I laughed.

"What's so funny?"

"I was just thinking about all the times I made fun of Brandon and some of the other guys when they got sappy with their girls. All that, 'you're so beautiful' stuff sounded so corny. But now..."

Taylor just smiled at me. We switched the topic since neither of us was comfortable with the present one. I wasn't all that big on discussing feelings and Tay was pretty shy on the subject. It didn't matter, we didn't need words to express how we felt. We could read it in each others eyes.

We chatted all the way home, about everything. We'd known each other such a short time, and yet, we talked like we'd been together for years.

4 Never a Moment Alone

Mom was in the kitchen when Tay and I came through the back door. I could read the question in her eyes. I rarely brought any of my friends home. We always seemed to hang out elsewhere. My parents weren't all that cool. There wasn't anything wrong with them exactly. I just didn't want my friends around them that much. Of course, all the guys pretty much felt that way about their parents.

"Mom, this is Tay."

"Tay, nice to meet you."

"It's nice to meet you Mrs. Bailey."

I could tell my mom liked Tay. He was polite and that got anyone my age on her good side real fast. He also had a "boy next door" clean-cut look that I knew my mom would like. He didn't have anything pierced either, so that was another mark in his favor. Her initial reaction to him was a good sign. I wanted my parents to like Taylor because I hoped he'd be around a lot.

I handed Tay a soda from the fridge and pulled him into the living room. We sat on the couch and watched a little MTV. Mom popped her head in and asked Tay to stay for supper. Taylor was really fitting in We lounged around for a bit watching videos. I was worn out from practice. I was starting to get sleepy. Before my eyelids grew too heavy, I fought it off and took Tay to my room. I closed the door behind us.

"Cool room." he said. He looked at all my trophies. "You must be really good at soccer." he said.

"I've been on some awesome teams." I replied, trying to be modest. I wasn't really very good at being modest. To be honest, I pretty much thought I was hot stuff on the soccer field. I should have been, I worked hard at it!

"From what I saw today, you're the one who's awesome." said Taylor.

"If you keep complimenting me, I'll have to say something about your looks!" I warned. "You want me to get sappy?"

"Okay, okay! I surrender." Taylor laughed. He couldn't stand up to my secret weapon, the compliment.

"What kind of music do you like?" I asked, flipping through my CD's, trying to find something I thought Tay would go for.

"I like just about everything, except country and western, rap, show tunes, and that opera crap. That shit makes me hurl!"

I laughed.

"No shit!" I said. "Someone could use opera to torture me for information. I'd spill my guts before I'd listen to that." I mimicked someone being interrogated, "I'll talk! I'll talk! I'll tell you everything! Just turn it off, please!"

I couldn't decide what CD to play, so I finally just pulled one out at random. I don't even remember which one it was. Tay said the music was cool. I have the feeling he would have said that if I put on some of that opera shit we were talking about, but he seemed to genuinely enjoy the music.

I flung myself on my bed and Tay sat beside me. I kept looking at him and thinking how attractive he was. I loved everything about him, even the way he was continually brushing the hair out of his eyes. He kept his long, blonde hair behind his ears as much as possible, but it just wouldn't stay. I loved his hair, it trailed down past his shoulders. I wished I could get my hair that long, but my parents practically threw a fit if it touched my shoulders. Every time it started looking cool, they made me get it cut. Parents!

Tay was handsome, but his looks were only part of what made him so appealing. His kind heart and cheery disposition made him all the more attractive, as did the fact that he seemed largely unaware of his own beauty. It was obvious I couldn't mention his looks however. It embarrassed him so much he turned red as a beet. I thought his extreme shyness made him look cuter still. I kept wanting to tell him how cute I thought he was, but I know it embarrassed him, so I tried to keep from saying anything about it. It wasn't easy.

Taylor's modesty about his looks really did make him more attractive. I knew some really good looking guys that were all hung up on themselves. It was obvious that they were really impressed with their own looks. They were always checking themselves out in the mirror and combing their hair just right. They reminded me of girls.

Some guys really got off on their own bodies. Some of the guys in my gym class, and a couple on the soccer team, were like that. They were always flexing their muscles while they watched themselves in the mirror. Those guys were conceited as hell. They were so impressed with themselves that it detracted from their looks.

Devon was kind of like that. He was a really good guy, but I could tell he thought he was really hot. I once suggested that he date himself since no one was as good looking as he was. I think he took it as a compliment. Anyway, Taylor was definitely not one of those guys, and I was glad.

I sat up. Being so near Taylor excited me. My heart was actually beating faster than normal, just because he was there. I really wanted to hug Tay, or hold his hand or something, but I was really a pretty shy guy, at least when it came to things like that. You'd never know it watching me on the soccer field or when I was playing football or basketball with my friends. I was a maniac when I played, but when I was alone with someone I was a different boy. After all, it wasn't like I was experienced. I'd never had a girlfriend (and never wanted one). Taylor was my first and only boyfriend. I was stumbling through virgin territory, if you'll forgive the pun. With Tay I was more shy than ever. I didn't want to do anything stupid. I didn't want to look foolish in front of him. I didn't give a damn about what the rest of the world might think, but I cared deeply about what Taylor thought of me. After what seemed like hours, I slowly reached out, grasped his hand, and held it. He looked down at my hand and smiled shyly.

I was sitting right beside Tay, about as close as one could imagine. The contact with his body sent my head spinning. I was keenly aware of everything about him. As we talked, my eyes drifted all over him. I noted every detail. I loved everything about him. It was hard to believe how happy I was, just because he was there.

The scent of Taylor's hair and cologne attracted me, everything about Taylor attracted me. We'd been talking the whole time we'd been sitting on the bed, but I don't remember much of what we said. I turned to Taylor, my eyes met his, and my words slowly trailed off into silence. We sat there just gazing into each others eyes. I felt as if our souls were communicating in a way we never could with words. Slowly, I raised my arms and wrapped them around him, drawing him closer still. He returned my embrace. We sat there and hugged. It was the greatest feeling I had ever experienced. I could feel his hot breath on my neck.

I could feel his heart pounding in his chest. I wanted to hold him forever and feel his strong arms around me.

"I feel so safe when you hold me." said Taylor softly. "I feel safe in a way I never have before."

He was safe. I'd protect him from anything. I'd die to protect him. Of that I had no doubt. I loved him and I'd do anything for him. Anything.

Taylor leaned back just a little and looked into my eyes.

"Mark, have you ever…" He paused. I could tell it was difficult for him to speak about what was on his mind. "This is tough." he said. I smiled.

"You can ask me anything Taylor, anything."

"Have you ever, you know, done anything with another guy?"

"Sure, lots!" I said.

Taylor looked kind of shocked. I laughed.

"In my dreams." I explained. "In real life, nothing, not once."

"You're evil!" he said. "You had me thinking all kinds of things."

"Have you ever…with a guy?" I asked.

"No, and not with a girl either. Well, I did kiss this one girl at my old school, or rather she kissed me. There were no tongues or anything."

"My cousin kissed me once." I said. "That's it for me, one quick kiss on the lips from my girl cousin."

"I guess we're officially virgins then." said Tay.

"Yeah, and I'm glad." I said. "I haven't been too happy about it in the past, but it's different now. Now it means that when we, you know, we'll both have our first time together."

Taylor smiled, and turned a little red. Talking about sexual matters was a lot harder alone in my bedroom than it was in a locker room full of guys. Well, you know what I mean. Talking about sex in the locker room was just bull-shitting, in my bedroom it was real.

"Uhm Mark?"

"Yeah?"

"Do you? You know?" The way Tay was so shy was really cute. I don't know how, but somehow I knew just what he was talking about.

"Do I jerk off?"

"Yeah."

"All the time." I said earnestly. "How could any guy not do that all the time?"

"Me too." he admitted.

Taylor was pretty embarrassed about the whole subject. I kind of was too. I knew it would get easier though, it was just going to take us a little time. All that talk about what we'd done, or in our case not done, with another guy was getting to me. It was getting hot in there.

We grew quiet and I hugged Taylor close to me once more. He nuzzled up against my cheek. I'd never dreamed that just hugging someone could make me so content. It was the most wonderful feeling in all the world. I was lost in the moment. I just sat there and enjoyed the closeness, love, and warmth. My God it was wonderful!

Mom knocked on the door and popped her head into my room.

"Supper's ready boys!" Mom was as cheerful as ever. She was gone as quickly as she came, but my heart was pounding in my chest. I practically shit my pants. Tay and I had released each other in a flash. Mom didn't suspect a thing, but it was way too close. What if she had caught us hugging? Like I wanted to explain something like that to my mother! Tay looked at me and shrugged with his eyes. I knew what he meant, being together was going to pose some interesting, and difficult problems.

I forgot all about the incident at supper. Dad was home and he seemed to like Tay as much as mom did. He quizzed him about his soccer team in Ohio and all sorts of sports stuff. I could tell mom was a little bored, but us three guys were having a great time. Sometimes I felt a little sorry for mom. Dad was a sports nut and I was a jock. Mom was always kind of outnumbered, and now, with Taylor, she was really outnumbered. She didn't seem to mind all that much. She had her own friends. Still, I bet she wished I had a sister.

I wished more than anything that I could introduce Tay to my parents as my boyfriend. I wanted to share with them my happiness, but I knew I'd never be able to do that. They would freak! Especially my father. He would go absolutely ape-shit if he knew his jock son was into guys. It made me a little sad to know I would never be able to share that part of my life with them, but I didn't let it take away from the happiness of the moment. Tay seemed like part of the family. It seemed that finally, everything was going just right.

Taylor was over at my house, or I at his, pretty much every day that week. Between soccer practice, homework, and the demands our parents made on us, we didn't really have much time alone together. We had time together, just not alone. Still, it was cool when Taylor hung out at my house. Having him in my living room, my kitchen, and my bedroom was as exciting to me as having some celebrity over. Even more so, I wasn't in love with any celebrity.

Hanging out at Tay's was cool too. His parents were typical parents I guess. Taylor's dad was a little heavy and looked like he was probably glued to the chair in the living room. Tay's mom was really nice, and really pretty. I wondered why she hooked up with someone like Taylor's father. Not that he wasn't attractive in his way, he just wasn't attractive compared to his wife. I could tell where Tay got his looks. His mom had beautiful blonde hair and the same blue-green eyes that Tay had. She had to be in her mid-thirties at least, but she looked like she was about twenty-three. Any other eighteen year old boy would have been drooling over her, but not me, I was interested in her son. Still, I could recognize beauty when I saw it. Tay's mom was hot!

I sure as hell didn't say that to Taylor. Of course, coming from me, he would have known it didn't mean anything. Still, I didn't want to make any waves so I kept quiet about it.

We spent as much time together as we could, but still it wasn't enough. Our time alone together was particularly rare. We did manage to hug a few times, and I sure liked that. I wanted more than anything to kiss Taylor, but he was shy by nature and I was shy about doing that sort of thing. I mean, I wanted to kiss him, but I just didn't want to push him too fast. I didn't want to do anything before he was ready. I knew I was probably being over cautious, but better that than ruin everything by being some kind of sex crazed maniac. Besides, the anticipation was enjoyable in itself. I wondered what it would be like. I found myself gazing at Taylor's lips, dreaming about the first time I would kiss him.

5 A New Life and New Troubles

The next Friday night there was a pep rally/hay ride at school. I always went to those things so it was natural that I be there. Tay met me there and we stuck to each other like glue. Not that we actually touched, that would have been too big a risk, but we were together every minute. Our team-mates had come to expect it. We were known already as close buds, but no one guessed the extent of our closeness. At least I hoped no one suspected how close we were. The fear of such suspicion had been playing on my mind more with each passing day. I didn't have a girl, and I was so tight with Taylor I was practically in his pocket. How long would Tay and I be able to avoid suspicion? I lived in fear of being found out. I tried not to think about it. I tried not to let it ruin my fun with Tay. But the fear was always there, lurking on the edge of my mind.

Andrea and her whole crowd were gathered around the large bon fire. As soon as Tay and I stepped into the glow of the flames, they were all over us. They flirted with us continuously. Andrea had been after my tail since grade school, but that evening she seemed more interested in Taylor, at least for the moment. She had a tendency to switch off onto other guys for a while, which always gave me a sense of relief. She never failed to work her way back to me however. I'd given her the "our friendship is too valuable to risk it by dating" line on more than one occasion. That generally kept her at bay for at least a few weeks. She always came back however and it was getting increasingly hard to put her off.

Andrea wasn't a problem for me at the bon fire. She was practically drooling over Taylor. Who could blame her? He was cute, athletic, sexy, and just plain hot. Andrea wasn't alone in her admiration for Taylor either. He was surrounded by girls hanging on his every word. There were a whole flock of them around us, gazing at us both with desire. Tay looked at me occasionally and smiled wanly. In a way, it was pretty funny that the girls were so hot after us. I mean, talk about wasting time. I almost felt bad for them, but hey, there were plenty of guys around that would be more than interested. Our followers would move on to some other hot hunks sooner or later. Most girls figured out I wasn't interested after a while and went in search of easier prey. Andrea never seemed to entirely give up. She'd leave for a while, but she was always back to try yet again.

To be honest, I liked the attention. It made me feel pretty good about myself that girls were hanging all over me, even if I wasn't interested in them. Just about any guy would like having girls look at him like that and have them say the things they said to me. I didn't mind when they were touching me either, it kind of made me feel hot. If that's as far as it went, having an admiring harem would have been cool, but sooner or later I was expected to choose one. That wasn't going to happen. I just wasn't interested in girls.

What would everyone think about that? I wasn't all that concerned with what others thought of me. Like I said before, I couldn't have cared less if someone didn't like my hair, my clothes, my music, or whatever. The possibility of others catching onto the fact that I was gay was quite another matter. I had to protect myself, and Tay. No guy in his right mind would turn down Andrea or any of her friends. Those babes were the hottest girls in school. They were hot after Tay and had been trailing me for a long time. It was only a matter of time before some of the guys wondered what was up. It wasn't natural for a teen-aged boy to turn down an opportunity like that. Andrea in particular had a reputation. I don't mean she was a slut or anything, but if she really liked a guy, she'd have sex with him. How many teen-aged boys do you know that would turn that down?

A couple of the guys on my soccer team had already ribbed me about not dating. One even said, "What, are you gay or something?" He was just kidding around, but I wondered how long would it be before someone seriously asked me that. I had been worried about arousing suspicions for some time. Hanging out with Taylor only intensified the danger.

Tay and I piled onto a hay wagon with our following of girls and some guys from our team. There were a lot of couples, but also just a lot of kids hanging out. I sat right by Tay. Andrea sat on his other side and Jennifer, a cute little blonde tennis player, cuddled up close to me. I wasn't happy at all about having Jennifer next to me. She was almost as bad as Andrea in her pursuit of me. I felt a little like a cornered beast.

Andrea and Jennifer were both getting a little aggressive. Andrea was touching Tay all the time and Jennifer grasped my arm and wouldn't let go. She even started feeling my biceps and asked if I worked out! Geesh! Any other guy would have been thrilled, but I found it awkward. Jennifer actually started feeling my chest through my shirt. I was about to push her hand away when I saw Devon looking at me. What guy would push away a hot blonde babe when she was after his bod?

Instead of pushing her away, I let her hands wander. I started flirting with her, putting on a show for Devon and whoever else might be watching. I rolled up my sleeve and flexed while she ran her hand over my hard biceps. I leaned over and nuzzled against her for a moment. It was a mistake. I knew immediately that I had fucked up. I had encouraged her. Before I knew what had happened, she kissed me. She grabbed me by the back of the head, pressed her lips hard against mine, and slipped her tongue into my mouth. I broke off the kiss as quickly as I could without looking like I was trying to break it off.

The situation was definitely getting out of hand. I was in a real spot, but what could I do about it? I still couldn't push her away, but I also couldn't let her think she was a potential girlfriend. She'd be wanting my class ring the next thing I knew. I had to put a stop to what was going on. Devon was still watching me and Jennifer, although he was pretending he wasn't. A couple of other guys were checking out the action too. No, I couldn't just push her away. But what could I do? I got an idea.

I guided Jennifer's hand back onto my chest, pulled up my shirt a little, then guided her fingertips down over my tight abs. She seemed to like that a lot. I noticed that Devon and a few of my other team-mates were watching harder than ever (while pretending even more that they weren't). I pushed Jennifer's hand lower and lower as I gazed into her eyes. I guided it over my belt buckle and right onto the bulge in my jeans. I was hard. It didn't have anything to do with Jennifer, but she didn't know that. Pressing her hand against my hard-on had the desired effect.

"Mark! What are you doing?"

I looked at her embarrassed. I wasn't acting. I really was embarrassed. I couldn't believe I'd really put her hand on my bulge, it just wasn't me. At least my plan worked however. After a momentary flair of her temper, Jennifer cooled down.

I was disappointed that she didn't leave me, but at least she wasn't quite as free with her hands. She contented herself with just sitting pressed up against me. I was pretty sure I could have had Jennifer if I'd played my cards right, and if that's what I'd wanted. I'd gambled that she'd pull back if I pushed her too fast. I don't know what I'd have done if I'd been wrong!

Devon and the guys that had been watching were snickering. They thought it was funny as hell. I could tell even Tay was struggling not to laugh. The guys couldn't control themselves and lost it. They tried to disguise their laughter by pretending they were laughing about something else. Jennifer bought it, but I knew what had cracked them up. I didn't mind that I'd made myself look really foolish. I had scored a few points with the guys. I had put on a little act that made them think I wanted a girl in my pants. Every little bit helped. They were laughing at me, but at the same time I know what I did impressed the hell out of them.

It was getting a little chilly, so all four of us burrowed into the hay. We were more hidden than exposed and it was kind of cozy in there. Tay's warm body pressed up next to mine filled me with warmth and contentment. My hand sought out his under the hay and soon our fingers were interlaced. He gave me a little squeeze and we sat there holding hands while the girls flirted with us.

Jennifer had backed off quite a bit and I thought I was safe, but then I felt her hand creeping to the very location she had so protested about earlier. Her hand was on my inner thigh, drawing ever closer to my manhood. Shit! My plan hadn't worked at all! Her reaction before was just an act for those around us. Was everyone just playing a part? Under the cover of the hay, her hands were beginning to wander and I didn't like where they were going.

Jennifer's actions weren't quite as hidden as she thought. Some of my teammates knew what she was up to, probably because they'd dated her before. I noticed some of them looking on with approval. Devon actually gave me the thumbs up when Jennifer wasn't looking. Ryan, our goalie, raised his eyebrows in an obvious "Way to go stud!" expression. There was nothing to do but play it up. Tay was actually kissing Andrea beside me. He sure as hell looked like he wanted in her pants. I pulled Jennifer close. For all the guys knew, Tay and I were both as interested in scoring with a girl as they were. The only problem was, it looked like both Taylor and I were about to succeed!

Jennifer was all over me, my little stunt before had the opposite of the desired effect. I thought I'd been so smart, but instead I'd put myself in a real spot. Jennifer didn't want to be a slut in public, but I was quickly getting the feeling she was one in private. She would have been another guy's dream come true (and I'm sure she had been). I was quickly learning that the rumors about her were true. I'd heard she was pretty damned easy, but I hadn't believed it, until she was all over me!

Jennifer ran her hand up under my shirt and felt my bare chest. She massaged my pecs. As the hay wagon rolled on, she inched her hand lower and lower. She slid it right over my abs and back onto the bulge in my jeans. I wasn't quite sure what to do. I didn't want to push her away, but I didn't want to encourage her either. I had tried that before and it backfired on me. What was happening between us wasn't going anywhere, but I had to at least act interested. What guy would discourage a girl when she was feeling him, there?

Tay was having similar problems with Andrea, she couldn't keep her hands to herself. I didn't blame her. I had trouble controlling myself around Tay as well. Hell, he was the reason I was excited, although I'm sure Jennifer thought it was her that was causing my jeans to tent. I squeezed Tay's hand under the hay once more. He squeezed back. I wondered if Andrea was trying to get into Tay's pants the way Jennifer was attempting to get into mine.

Shit! Jennifer actually unfastened my belt and unbuttoned my jeans. I was panicking. Things were going way, way too far. Jennifer slipped her hand into my boxers. I couldn't believe what was happening. What she was doing with her hand felt real good, and I felt guilty for liking it. I felt like I was cheating on Tay or something. It wasn't like I had a choice however. My friends were watching. They knew what was going on under the hay. I couldn't make her stop. Mmmm, it did feel good. Jennifer's hand slid up and down, up and down. She might be a girl, but it didn't matter when she was touching me like that.

I started breathing a little harder. Jennifer's hand was driving me out of my mind. No one had ever touched me like that before. I had to fight hard to keep quiet and to keep still. Jennifer looked into my eyes. She had this real wicked, mischievous look on her face. I know she thought no one around us had a clue as to what she was doing, but she couldn't have been more wrong as far as Devon, Ryan, and a handful of my friends were concerned.

What she was doing felt real good, but at the same time I didn't want it. I felt kind of violated. It was almost like I was being raped or something. Sure, I could have made her stop at any time, but I couldn't really do that. I had to avoid suspicion. There was no way out. I felt like I was wasting my first time, but what was going on didn't exactly count. I tried to force the pleasure from my mind. I didn't want to like it. It made me feel like I was betraying Taylor and that was the worst feeling in all the world.

I couldn't take it any more. Jennifer was driving me crazy. My eyes rolled back into my head and I moaned softly. I hadn't felt anything that incredible in a long, long time. It was so much better than when I did that to myself. It seemed ten times more powerful and intense. A wave of pleasure surged through my entire body.

The guys were watching me. Devon was actually snickering. He knew exactly what was going on. I knew that on Monday morning, I'd be hearing a lot about Jennifer getting me off. All the guys would be talking about it. At least that much good would come of it. I hated what had happened, but it would help camouflage my relationship with Taylor.

The release of sexual tension felt awesome, but as soon as I was finished, I felt this great mass of guilt descend upon me. I felt like shit. I felt like I'd sacrificed myself to hide my relationship with Taylor. I'd done something I did not want to do, to hide a love I wished I could share with the world. I felt so used, and so guilty, but then again, was there really any way for me to get out of what had just happened? If there was, I sure didn't know how. It wasn't like I'd tried to get Jennifer to give me a hand-job. It was all her idea. Still, I felt guilty as hell about the whole thing, especially since it had felt so damned good!

Mercifully, the hay wagon stopped, the ride was over. If only it could have ended a few minutes earlier! I buttoned up my jeans and fastened my belt. The only good thing about the whole incident was that Devon, Ryan, and a couple others witnessed the whole thing. At least that bought me a little protection. I kept repeating that to myself, trying to make myself feel better about the whole thing. It didn't help much.

Jennifer pulled me to the side as we slipped off the wagon.

"Mark, would you like to go somewhere more... private?"

Every other boy's dream was my nightmare. Jennifer wanted me and wanted me bad. What had happened in the wagon was only the beginning. My mind raced for a way out.

"Jennifer, I'd like to, what guy wouldn't? But..."

"But what?" she pouted.

I was wondering "but what?" too. Shit! What was I going to do?

"No one knows it yet, but I'm kind of seeing someone." It wasn't a lie, but it wasn't exactly the truth either.

"Who?" she demanded.

"I can't tell you." Now that was the truth!

"Who is she?"

"Sorry Jennifer, I just can't tell."

"You bastard! You used me! All you guys just want the same thing! Why didn't you tell me?" Suddenly we had everyone's attention. Just what I didn't want. I wished I could just turn invisible. Jennifer was yelling at me and everyone was looking at us.

I thought Jennifer was being pretty hypocritical. I mean, she was the one that worked her hands into my pants. She was the one who wanted exactly what she accused me of being after. Hell, if I hadn't turned her down, I bet she'd have done anything I wanted, anything.

"What was I supposed to do? You were all over me!" I was getting angry, her whole attitude was pissing me off. I felt like she'd used me.

"Fuck you Mark!"

Jennifer slapped my face hard. Everyone watched as she stomped off in a huff. She was not happy at all. I couldn't tell if she was pissed because I'd let her do what she did, or because she wasn't going to get to do any more, or both. At least she was gone.

Once the show was over, everyone went back to their business. I knew they were all talking about me however. It was attention I did not need.

Taylor had managed to disentangle himself from Andrea with far more grace. At least he hadn't created a major scene. At any rate, he was walking toward me alone. We quietly slipped away from the crowd. We didn't speak until we were well out of earshot.

"I really handled that well!" I said sarcastically, rolling my eyes.

"Well," said Taylor, "at least I don't think she'll be after you anymore."

"No shit!"

Taylor laughed.

"What did you tell Andrea?"

"I just told her you were my boyfriend."

He said it so seriously that I actually believed him for a moment. I was shocked, the color drained from my face, and my mouth was hanging open. Tay burst out laughing.

"Arggggh!" I growled and mock punched him in the stomach. "Don't do that! You scared the shit out of me!" That just made Taylor laugh more. He really had frightened me. My heart was pounding in my chest. I laughed too, in relief.

Tay and I walked along the same forest path I had followed the night we met. The cross country team used those paths for practice, but on a Friday night they were devoid of life. There were no girls, no team-mates. We could be alone. At least I hoped so, if we came there for privacy, might not another couple do the same?

"What are we going to do about this?" I asked seriously. "We can't keep pushing girls away without anyone getting suspicious."

"You didn't look like you were pushing Jennifer away." said Tay.

It was dark, but he could still see the look of guilt on my face. I told him what had happened. His eyes were filled with understanding, and compassion.

"Hey, Mark, I know. I was sitting right beside you, remember? We were so close she was practically in my pants. Listen, I didn't like what happened, but what could you do, punch her in the face for something? Forget about it. It's over. It doesn't matter."

"I just don't want to hurt you Taylor. I'd never do anything to hurt you. I..." I felt so bad that I was on the verge of tears. Taylor grasped my chin and pulled my face up so he could look into my eyes.

"I know Mark." he said softly. "And you didn't, okay?" I nodded.

"I love you Taylor." His understanding made me feel so good inside.

"I love you too Mark."

We stood there for a moment, then walked on.

"What are we going to do about this? Everyone's bound to get suspicious and I don't want to go through another night like this one again."

"I don't know Mark. I've been thinking the same thing." said Tay.

"Did you see Jennifer on me? Right before she slapped me, she asked me to take her somewhere private. She didn't come right out and say it, but I think she was going to blow me, I think she wanted fucked."

"Really?" said Tay. "Of course, after doing what she'd already done, I guess that shouldn't surprise me. Andrea was wanting me to take her out by the bleachers. I don't think she had anything quite that involved in mind, but still..."

"You know word's going to get around that we didn't do anything with them." I said. "Well, that we didn't do anything more than we did anyway."

"I know."

"Shit, the guys have already been on me. They're going to wonder what's going on. I mean, no guy would turn down Jennifer unless..."

"He's gay." Tay finished for me.

"The guys sure were watching us on the hay-ride. Devon gave me a thumbs up! I guess I kind of blew that however, turning down Jennifer right in front of him."

"At least we put on a good act, even if we didn't take it as far as we could have."

"If only we could keep up that act." I said.

Taylor paused, clearly turning something over in his mind.

"Why not?" asked Tay.

"Huh?" I didn't quite understand.

"Why can't we keep up the act? We could date girls so no one would suspect us, and still date each other on the sly."

"Tay, Jennifer was all over me. There's no way I could date her! If I act like she's my girlfriend, I'll have to really have sex with her. And I don't think you'll be able to keep Andrea at bay long either. That girl has it for you bad."

"I didn't mean those two!." said Tay. "We need nice girls, you know, ones that aren't about to go any further than making out without some major commitment. We need girls that don't put out."

"I don't know if I'd feel right about that. I mean, I'd feel like some kind of tease."

"Just don't promise anything you can't give. Look, we take them out, show them a good time, have fun. We pay attention to them at school, hold hands with them, that sort of thing. We make out with them a little and that's all. Before it gets real serious we can cool things down, break up even. No one will get hurt."

I had doubts, but I pushed them from my mind.

"I guess so. I guess it wouldn't hurt. I mean, we would be showing them a good time."

"Yeah, and we can double date and be together at the same time. It's the perfect cover. We can see each other a lot with our girls, and still spend time alone with each other."

"We're alone now." I said. The topic at hand was important, but I had other things on my mind.

Tay stopped and smiled at me sweetly. We looked at each other in the pale blue moonlight. Tay was so handsome with his beautiful blonde hair flowing down over his blue and white sweater. Taylor looked so good in sweaters, but then he looked good in anything.

I wrapped my arms around him and drew him close. His strong arms pulled me hard against him. I could feel his warmth, feel his heart beating in his chest.

I nuzzled against his neck, drinking in the delicate scent of his hair and his cologne. I sighed, completely relaxed. We just stood there hugging each other for a few moments on the dark forest path. It was one of those moments that I wished could last forever.

I leaned back and gazed into Taylor's eyes, they sparkled with the light of the stars. We inched forward, our faces drawing ever so slowly closer, our eyes gazing at each other dreamily. Time had no meaning. The moments stretched into eternity. My lips neared his for minutes, hours, ages. Taylor was my whole world, and I his. This was it. This was love. I pressed my lips to his and we kissed, delicately, then more deeply. It was our first kiss and one that will remain forever etched in my mind.

We dared not stay alone in the woods for long. We had been gone too long already and soon suspicions would arise. I hoped no one had seen us slip away. I could just image the rumors after that. Everyone would be talking about how I turned Jennifer down, then slipped into the woods with Taylor. Yeah, that would be real pleasant!

Reluctantly, our lips parted, we broke our embrace, and headed back toward the bonfire, hand in hand. I could still taste Taylor's sweet kiss. My mind was filled with his presence. Warmth flowed through our clasped hands. Simply touching him, having him near, brought me a contentment that was beyond description. I couldn't think of anything more wonderful than being in love. Only when we drew near the light did I release Taylor's hand. His mere touch filled my heart with bliss.

6 Web of Deceit

At last Taylor and I had a plan that would protect us, and I already had a couple of girls in mind. Even before we reached the bonfire, I discussed the possibilities with Tay. When we arrived, his girl was there, as was mine. I pushed Tay in the direction of his future "girlfriend" and headed for mine before Jennifer could locate me and attach herself. She'd left me in a huff, but I had the feeling she'd be back.

I felt just a little guilty as I approached Laura, after all my intentions were not pure. But then again, were the intentions of any eighteen year old boy toward a girl pure? Most boys my age would have been hot after the very thing I sought to avoid. Wouldn't most girls be thrilled with a handsome young man who would pay attention to her, tell her how beautiful she was, buy her affectionate gifts, and show her a good time - all without pressuring her for sex?

Perhaps what I was offering was exactly what Laura needed. Still, there was this little bit of guilt in the pit of my stomach that just wouldn't go away. I knew in my heart that what I was doing was wrong, no matter how pleasant I intended to make the lie, it was just that, a lie. I could never be the kind of boyfriend of which girl's dreamed. It just wasn't possible. I pushed my doubts and guilt to the side and forged ahead. I had to do it. It was a matter of self-preservation. Taylor and I had to avoid suspicion and taking on fake girlfriends was the only way to do it. There was just no other way.

Laura was standing with a couple of friends. She eyed me shyly as I approached. I could read excitement and a touch of admiration in her eyes, just like at the dance. She lit up as I neared. She had the look of someone who had within her grasp what she'd always wanted, and yet feared that it would slip away. I realized how badly I could hurt her if I wasn't careful. It scared me. Having that kind of responsibility over another person's life was frightening. I knew what lie ahead wasn't going to be easy. Along with the guilt, there were butterflies in my stomach. I had to fight to keep my voice even.

"Laura?" I inquired as sweetly as I could, making it plain that something was on my mind. I hadn't paid much attention to her at the dance. I wanted her to think that it was because I was shy, not because I wasn't interested. I wanted her to believe that it had taken me a few days to work up the courage to approach her.

"Mark, hi." she said turning from her friends. The girls near her watched our exchange intently. I felt like I was acting in a play before an audience. I guess I was in a way. I nervously pushed the hair out of my eyes.

"Hi." I said, in my best "shy" voice.

Laura was kind of shy, for real, and obviously excited I was paying attention to her. She had seemed much more outgoing at the dance. I guess it was harder for her with me standing right there talking to her.

"There's a dance tomorrow night." I said. "I was wondering if you'd like to go with me?" Asking her out wasn't easy. I was so nervous. I guess all guys felt that way when they asked out a girl.

"I'd like that Mark."

"Tomorrow then, say seven?"

"Sure."

I almost left without getting her address, duh! I wasn't good at interacting with a girl at all. I heard Laura and her girlfriends start chatting as soon as they thought I was out of ear-shot. All I caught was "He's so cute!" It made me feel real good about myself for a moment, but then the feeling melted away and I felt wicked and deceitful. No, I didn't feel good about what I was doing at all.

Jennifer observed what went on as well and she wasn't happy, not at all. I could tell she was pissed. I don't think she overheard what Laura and I said, but she may have suspected that I lied to her when I told her I was seeing someone else. Of course, I wasn't really lying. I was seeing Taylor, but she'd think it was a lie all the same if she discovered I'd just asked out Laura. Either way, she was mad as hell. It was probably just as well, maybe it would get her off me once and for all. If she thought I was a jerk it might finally break the spell that seemed to attract her to me. Maybe she'd tell Andrea too and I could be rid of her as well.

I couldn't help but feel awkward about the whole situation. What was I getting myself into?

What a web of deception and deceit Taylor and I were weaving. Fake girl-friends, a hidden love, and who knew what was to come. And yet, we had little choice in the matter. Our parents, our friends, hell most of the world would have disowned us if the truth were known. For all the talk of acceptance and under-standing, there was still a great deal of prejudice and hate out there. What kind of world was it where loving a member of your own sex was treated like such a crime? Why couldn't everyone understand that love was a wonderful thing, no matter who loved who? Some of my classmates even believed that homosexuals went straight to hell. Now what kind of thinking was that? Go to hell for caring about someone, for loving someone? I don't think so!

Despite being coerced into deceit by a cold-hearted world, I didn't feel good about it. I had never liked the idea of lying. Sure, I told my mom her new hair style looked great sometimes when it didn't, or I told one of my friends his new CD was cool when I didn't really care that much for it, but basically I was an honest person. Besides, lying required a sharp memory. I had enough trouble remembering everything that really did happen. I didn't need the hassle of remembering something fictional. Lies had a way of building on themselves too. It usually took one lie to cover up the first, then another, and another. Pretty soon there were nothing but lies. I hated the very idea. I didn't like what Tay and I were forced into doing at all, but there was nothing to do, but make the best of it.

I was a little taken aback, and momentarily hurt, when Laura and I stepped into the gym. Taylor and his girl Stephanie were already on the dance floor. It was a slow dance and Tay was holding Steph as close as could be. He was smil-ing at her, laughing, and clearly enjoying himself. I was actually jealous for a moment, but then I came to my senses. I thought to myself that maybe the whole girlfriend act would work, it even fooled me for a moment.

I took Laura's hand and smiled at her.

"Care to dance?"

She laughed sweetly and let me pull her onto the dance floor. I wrapped my arms around her and held her close. She nuzzled up against my neck as we danced and told me how kind and thoughtful I was. Her compliment tore at me like a barb in my flesh. I was glad she couldn't see my face. I have no doubt the shame and remorse I was experiencing were clear to read upon my features. My face was a book that told a tale of deception and deceit. I pushed the guilt out of my mind and struggled to smile, not for the last time.

Despite the feeling of guilt in my gut, I was beginning to have fun. I loved the music and I loved moving in time to it. It was almost as if the music and I were one and the same. I felt like I was inside it, or it was inside of me, that I was a part of it, or it a part of me. I loved the feel of my own body as I danced in rhythm with the music. I'd always felt the most in touch with myself while I was doing something physical. I loved to think and contemplate, but I always did that best when I was doing something with my body. It was as if my mind needed my body to think. I felt and thought with my muscles. When I walked, my thoughts followed a path just like my feet. When I ran, my thoughts raced along with me. When I danced as I was dancing with Laura, my mind intermixed with the world around me. It's all rather difficult to explain.

Laura and I moved around the dance floor, now fast, now slow. We were surrounded by friends and class-mates. It was as if my whole world were in the gym. I guess it was my whole world, at least the world that I knew. I knew other places existed, I'd visited many of them, but Verona, Indiana was still pretty much my entire world. I looked around me and took it all in at a glance. My world had not looked so beautiful in quite a long time.

As much as I enjoyed dancing with Laura, I couldn't keep my eyes off Taylor. I wasn't jealous, even though he seemed to be having an awesome time. It wasn't that at all. I kept gazing at him, thinking how wonderful he was and how lucky I was that he was my boyfriend. I had dreamed of having someone to love, and someone to love me in return. I had been granted that, and more. Looks didn't really matter all that much to me. Well, yes, they mattered, but there were other things far more important. I would have been happy with a kind, ordinary guy, but I'd been given someone not only as wonderful as could be, but incredibly handsome as well. I couldn't believe my good luck. At last, things were going my way. Taylor and I were going through a lot to be together, but it was worth it.

My friends danced around me, holding their girls tight. For the first time, I felt like I belonged. I didn't feel like an outsider watching life from afar. I didn't feel like a vampire hiding from the light of day. I felt like just one of the guys. I knew it was but an illusion. I knew that I was indeed a vampire. But was there really that much difference between fantasy and reality? Five hundred years ago, a lot of people thought the world was flat. That was a fantasy, but yet many lived out their lives in that fantasy without even questioning it. Who knew how much of what we accepted as reality today would be shown to be mere fantasy in the future. Perhaps all of life was a fantasy, an illusion, did that mean we should not live it? For once in my life I enjoyed feeling just like everyone else. It was a fantasy, and it might not live long, but at least I could enjoy it before it was gone.

The air was filled with the rhythm of the music and something more. The dancers created a special aura. It's hard to describe, but there seemed something magical about the night. This night was so very different from that of two weeks before when I first met Tay. I stood on the fringe then, present, but not really a part of things. Dancing with Laura, I felt as if I fit in.

Tay pushed his hair out of his eyes and caught me looking at him. He smiled at me. In that brief look I could read his thoughts. He was having fun, but he would have much rather been dancing with me. Our thoughts were one. If only we could have danced together with all our friends! If only we could have held each other close, surrounded by our class-mates, without fear of anyone hating us for it. How wonderful that would be! A sadness touched my heart that my dream would never come true. I gazed at Tay with love in my eyes, and read the same in his in return. The world might not be as we desired, but Taylor and I were all that we could have wished. Taylor was my wish come true.

As I was watching Taylor with dreamy eyes, I became aware that Laura was speaking to me.

"I'm sorry Laura, what did you say?"

"I was saying how beautiful all this is, with the lights, and the decorations."

"Oh, yes, it is that. I was just noticing it myself. It makes my mind drift away."

Laura put her head on my shoulder. I held her as if protecting her, although probably I should have been protecting her from me. My dishonestly left a bitter taste on my tongue. Laura was certainly a sweet girl and lovely too in her way. I was sorry that I couldn't be for her all that she wanted me to be. I felt like I was cheating her of her dreams.

The song ended and the next one was wild and fast. The whole mood of the room changed from dreamy to out of control. I think I liked the wildness even better, it allowed me to clear my head and just be physical. Laura and I went crazy, our legs and arms flailing in rhythm with the beat. I found myself laughing out loud and Laura was giggling at how crazy I was acting. It was so much fun! As much as I loved it, I had rarely danced before. I realized what I had been missing. I wished yet again that Tay and I could dance together. Why could the world not at least allow us that?

By the end of the dance I was nearly out of breath. Laura and I relinquished the floor to our tireless classmates. Taylor led Steph over to the refreshment table where we each grabbed a soda for our dates.

"What up Tay?"

"Hey, Mark, I think you know my girlfriend, Steph?"

"Girlfriend?" I said, as if surprised. I found I was pretty good at acting. "Hi Steph." I gave her an affectionate hug. I knew her well. We'd been friends since grade school.

"Hey Mark, I said my girlfriend, not yours!" said Tay with mock anger.

I laughed.

"For your information, I already have one." I shot back. "Tay, this is Laura."

All four of us talked and caught our breath. I could feel eyes peering at us. There were team-mates looking on with approval, Jennifer glaring with anger from afar, and even teacher's noticing me with a girl for the first time. There was an overall sense of approval, like I'd passed some kind of test. I fit in with Verona, Indiana's narrow sense of how things should be.

As good as "fitting in" felt, I couldn't shake the sense of somehow being a traitor to what I was. I felt like I was too big of a coward to stand up for what I believed. I was enjoying the sense of approval, when I should have been dancing with Taylor, challenging the world to disapprove if it dared. I wasn't living up to my ideal self. Living up to that ideal was far harder in reality than it was in mere thought however. I could not live openly as I wished. I had to live in secrecy. That was the way it had to be. I had to live the life of a vampire. I just wasn't brave enough to live openly as what I was. The world made that far too difficult and dangerous a task.

Soon, it was back to the dance floor. We could talk anytime, but dances were not so common. The dance was a slow one, I held Laura close as we danced, and talked.

"Taylor's very handsome isn't he?" said Laura.

"Thinking of switching boyfriends?" I chided.

"No! You're very handsome too, but isn't he?"

"I have to admit, he is." If only Laura knew just how attractive I found Tay.

"They make such a cute couple." said Laura. Her conversation was boring me a little. To be honest, I'd rather have been talking about music, or soccer, or horse-back riding. That's one thing I liked about having a boyfriend, we could talk about guy stuff all the time. There was none of that 'How's my hair look?', 'What do you think of this outfit?', or 'Does this make me look fat?' crap. Sure, guys care about how they look, but they don't go on and on about it, and they don't spend time talking about how cute other couples are. Yuck! I think one of the reasons I was attracted to guys was that I so enjoying being one. There was just something special about being male. There was a lot to admire in maleness. Women just didn't cut it where I was concerned. Not that there was really anything wrong with them, they just weren't guys.

By the end of the night my feet were tired and I felt like I'd been through a rough soccer practice. Why was it that dancing wore me out more than running? No matter, it was great fun in any case. I hadn't had such a good time in I don't know how long. Laura really enjoyed herself too. I was very pleased about that. I wanted to make sure that Laura always had a good time when she was with me. I owed her that. I knew I could never really make up for the deceit, but I wanted to come as close to it as I possibly could. I bid Taylor an affectionate goodbye, then departed with Laura on my arm. How different things were from the way I wanted them to be.

I drove Laura home, ill at ease over what she expected of me. It was funny in a way. I was experiencing the same feelings as other boys, but for entirely different reasons. Other boys would have been all nervous because they were dying for a kiss, hopefully one involving tongues. I was apprehensive because I feared Laura would want to kiss me. I sought to avoid precisely what other boys craved.

I walked Laura up the worn steps that led to her house and affectionately hugged her at the door. I was nervous, my stomach was filled with butterflies. Did she expect me to kiss her? If so, was I supposed to use my tongue? Being with a girl was all alien territory to me. I knew if I did too little it would hurt her. She'd think I didn't find her attractive, that she wasn't pretty. If I tried too much, she'd get mad and accuse me of having only one thing on my mind. Girls were so hard to figure out!

I was saved by Laura's little brother staring at us through the living room window. That drew the attention of Laura's mother and our privacy was gone. I was spared the awkwardness of a kiss, at least for the moment. As Laura went inside, I departed, as quickly as I dared. Laura's mom had a rule that she had to meet Laura's dates. I had lucked out when I picked Laura up, her mom was gone. I didn't feel like dealing with her at the end of our date. Too many things were going through my mind. She did not pursue me however. I released a sigh of profound relief, for escaping Laura's mother, and the awkwardness of a kiss. Most boys would have been annoyed and frustrated by such an interruption. I was thrilled. I felt like I had been saved at just the last moment. But what about the next time we went out? Once again, I wondered just what I'd gotten myself into.

7 Acceptance and Guilt

Our little ploy was already beginning to have the desired effect. Guys were punching me in the shoulder in the halls at school. I heard "Way to go stud!" more times than I could count. It was all typical teen-aged boy stuff and highly exaggerated. It did feel good to be getting that kind of attention from my classmates however. I was accustomed to quite a bit of attention, but not like that. Tay and I had entered the world of guys who had girlfriends. It was the perfect cover for guys who had boyfriends.

Devon really pissed me off just before soccer practice however. I had no problem with the enthusiasm of the other boys over my "girl", but I didn't appreciate crude remarks. The guys were ohhing and ahhing over Laura when Devon had to go too far.

"Hey Mark, does Laura give good head?" he yelled across the locker room. I reacted with genuine anger to that. Laura may not have really been my girlfriend, but she was a friend and I felt responsible for her reputation. Everyone knew a lot of the girls at our school gave head. Hell, that made those particular girls really popular. Laura wasn't like that however and it just didn't seem right for Devon to say that about her.

"Laura's not a slut like the girls you date!" I snapped before I even knew what I was saying. The whole locker room grew deathly still. Our words could have been the preamble to a major fight, but Devon and I were pretty good friends. He knew he had gone just a little too far, and he knew I was pissed. I was overreacting, but once I got mad about something I didn't have much self control. I was not someone to mess with if my anger was aroused.

"Hey, dude, I'm sorry" said Devon. "I didn't mean anything. I was just, you know..." I could tell by the tone of his voice his apology was sincere. My anger was immediately quelled. I might over-react pretty easily sometimes, but I was also quick to forgive. I held Devon's gaze for a moment, just to make sure he knew he'd come real close to getting his ass kicked, then I let him up easy.

"It's okay Devon. I'm sorry I blew up like that. It's just that Laura's a really nice girl and I don't want anyone saying stuff like that about her."

"Hey, I understand. Let's just forget about it. I think pretty highly of Laura too. I asked her out once and she shot me down!"

"Like all the girls!" shouted one of our team-mates. That started a towel fight and the room was filled with half naked young jocks snapping each other with towels. What a beautiful sight.

The little scene between me and Devon served my purpose well, even though it was far from planned. Now all the guys knew I really cared about Laura. It wasn't an act either. She was not my girl, but I considered her my friend. To me, friendship really meant something. I did care for her, just not the way my friends thought. If I hadn't cared for her, maybe I could have shaken the cloud of guilt that was always hovering just overhead.

The whole fake girlfriend situation concerned me a great deal. It didn't bother me too much to lie about having a girlfriend to my team-mates and class-mates. Most of the stuff guys said about what they did with girls was bullshit anyway. I'd be willing to bet that there were far more virgins in my gym class and on my soccer team than any of the guys would admit. I'd wager not one of them got as much action as he claimed. You'd think from the way they talked that most of them did nothing but have sex. Most of them probably did have a lot of sex, but I'm sure it involved only their own hand.

It didn't cause me too much grief to lie to the guys, but what about Laura and Steph? I considered both of them friends. Taylor and I were taking advantage of them. No matter how nice we were about it, nothing could alter that fact. I didn't feel very good about lying to Laura. I hadn't exactly promised to date her until we got married, but still, I knew she was expecting more than I could give. Withholding that information was too much like lying for my tastes. It went against my beliefs. I had a sense of guilt in my gut that just would not go away, no matter how hard I tried to rationalize the situation. No matter how much fun

Laura had, no matter what I did for her, it didn't alter the fact that I was leading her on. I made her think she had a boyfriend when she really didn't. I just couldn't get what I was doing out of my mind.

Laura was really happy however. She lit up whenever she saw me in the halls at school. She smiled at me sweetly and squeezed me tight when I hugged her. I caught a few looks from other girls. They envied Laura. They wanted what she had. That made me feel pretty good about myself. It was nice to be wanted. Would they envy her if they knew the truth however? I didn't think so. Even Laura's happiness made me feel guilty. I knew she was happy about something that just wasn't real. I knew she was living in a fantasy that I had created. If the fantasy held, it would be just as good as reality for her, but what if it didn't hold? How long could I make it real for her? Eventually, our relationship had to end. When the time came, could I do it in such a way to preserve the fantasy? Could I make our entire relationship a pleasant memory of things that just didn't quite work out in the end? How was I going to bring that off? How did I get myself into such a mess? There was no backing out however. I had to go on.

That whole week after the dance, Tay and I were the talk of the school. You'd think there would be more interesting things to talk about, but who was going with who was always the big topic. Tay and I hooking up with girlfriends was the very latest news and the gossip was flying. It even overshadowed the whole incident with Jennifer. The attention was kind of a pain, and yet, I enjoyed it as well. I guess it was my fifteen minutes of fame. In a week or so, some new couple would step into the spotlight, either by hooking up, or breaking up, but for the moment, we were it.

Our objective was certainly accomplished. Taylor and I had drawn a cloak of secrecy around us that prevented anyone from guessing what we really were. The villagers did not suspect they had vampires in their midst. Everyone believed Tay and I had girlfriends. The focus was now on me and Laura, and Tay and Steph, rather than on me and Tay. All doubts about us were erased. No one was wondering about our close friendship. We were on the same soccer team and our girlfriends were close friends. It only stood to reason that we'd be spending a lot of time together too. Besides, there was nothing wrong with having close male friends. Our "girlfriends" kept the suspicions that would have arisen at bay. Homosexuals didn't have girlfriends, everyone knew that. We could spend as much time with each other as we wanted and no one would give it a second thought. That was an incredible asset, but it was bought at a terrible cost.

With our new "girlfriends" came the additional problem of finding time alone together. Finding time to be alone was always a hassle and our girls only increased the difficulty. I don't know how many evenings I spent with Laura when I really wanted to be alone with Tay. It was so frustrating!

Taylor and I spent quite a bit of time together; in classes, between classes, at lunch, at soccer practices, and at soccer games. We were always surrounded by others however. Our conversations were necessarily censored by those around us. There was no chance to speak freely and no chance to be intimate in the least. I longed to just hold Tay's hand, or give him a hug, but it was all but impossible. We could have had a little privacy at Taylor's house, or mine, but when we weren't busy with school or soccer, our girlfriends demanded our time. I couldn't get over how needy girls were. If I didn't spend time with Laura every evening, and then call her at night, she accused me of not caring about her. Why did she constantly have to be reassured? It was driving me out of my mind! I mean, give me a break.

Even though we were rarely alone, I valued every moment with Taylor. From the very start Tay and Steph double dated with me and Laura. I guess it was really a triple date. I mean, there was Taylor and Stephanie, me and Laura, and me and Taylor. I wasn't all that experienced with dating. Okay, I wasn't experienced at all. Most of the time we all just kind of hung out together. I had trouble thinking of things to do for more formal dates. We'd already done the dance thing for our first real date, so we all went to the movies for the second. That's what couples seemed to always be doing.

I was nervous about picking up Laura at her house. I just knew her mother would be waiting on me. Any boy that wanted to date Laura had to pass inspection. I had lucked out on our first date, but I knew I'd have to meet her sooner or later. I was actually hoping she would be home so I could put the experience behind me. I never liked to put unpleasant things off. I'd rather get them over with and be done with it.

At least I wouldn't have to endure an awkward scene with Laura's father. Her dad had taken off when she was in kindergarten and hadn't been seen since. After the stories my friends had told me, I was glad I didn't have her father to deal with. Most fathers looked over their daughter's dates like they were sizing up a piece of beef at the supermarket. Without exception they seemed to think that the boys that came to take their daughters out were sex-crazed maniacs or something. Of course, that was a pretty good description of most boys my age.

I guess it was a pretty good description of me in a way. Sometimes I felt like a sex crazed maniac. Sometimes I felt like I was ready to explode with desire. None of that desire was directed at Laura however. Her mother had nothing to worry about.

I pulled up in front of Laura's house. I was so nervous my stomach ached a little. My heart was pounding in my chest like I'd just ran a mile. I laughed at myself for getting so worked up over nothing. I walked up the steps. The door seemed like a gateway to some dangerous realm. I knocked. Moments later Laura's mom opened the door. She was very attractive, for a woman in her thirties anyway.

"Mark isn't it?" she asked.

"Yes. Hi."

"I'm Katie. Come on in Mark. Laura isn't ready yet. It'll give us a chance to talk."

The moment I'd been dreading had come. It figured that Laura wouldn't be ready, even though I was exactly on time. If she'd been in the room with me, enduring her mother's questioning would have been easier. Laura had never been ready on time yet. What was it with girls anyway? Didn't they know how to tell time?

Laura's mom ushered me into the living room and we sat facing each other, mere inches apart. We were so close to each other, it made me uncomfortable. There was no where to hide. She seemed very nice, and that put me at ease a bit, but I was still nervous.

"So Mark, tell me about yourself."

It had arrived. The moment of truth. I wasn't quite sure what to say, so I told her about what I was doing at school. I talked a lot about soccer too. I tended to do that, talk about soccer that is. I was so enthused about it that sometimes I couldn't think about anything else. Talking about soccer made me much more comfortable.

Katie asked a lot of questions, but she seemed genuinely interested, instead of suspicious. I knew I was there on approval, but I had the feeling I was passing with ease. My nervousness about meeting Laura's mom was quickly dissipating, but something new was troubling my mind. I found myself growing wary, even though I felt silly about it at the same time. The suspicion creeping into my thoughts was too absurd to be true.

Katie looked me over as we talked. I'd expected that. I knew I was being sized up. There was something peculiar in the way she looked at me however, something that kind of disturbed me. I was beginning to suspect there was something to her gaze that wasn't quite pure. There was something in her eyes. Was it hunger? Desire? I had the feeling she wasn't checking me out for Laura's sake, she was just checking me out. The more she looked at me, and the more I thought about it, the more uncomfortable I became.

I knew I was probably being stupid. What would a woman in her thirties want with a eighteen year old boy? That thought gave me pause. I was far from naïve. I knew exactly what such a woman might want. I looked into her eyes and I knew I was right. Laura's mom had the hots for me!

That realization made me really nervous. It was kind of flattering, but kind of creepy too. It was nothing like when the girls at school flirted with me. It didn't even feel the same as when Jennifer put her hand down my pants. It was totally different. I was more than half afraid that she was going to touch me, somewhere I didn't want to be touched. I felt like I was in one of those situations where the best thing to do was run away, but this wasn't a stranger offering me candy to coax me into her car, this was my girlfriend's mother!

Katie didn't really do anything except look at me, but the way she did it made me feel like she wanted me. I knew I was probably being stupid, but I was still uncomfortable. It was so unexpected, that I didn't even notice what was going on for a long time. Once I caught on however, her desire for me was pretty damn clear. As we talked, her eyes roamed over me, lingering on my shoulders, arms, and chest. She even glanced down at my crotch a few times. She was always very subtle. I'm not even sure if I was meant to know she was checking me out. She was making me really uncomfortable however. I felt like I'd stepped into an after school special.

The whole situation blew my mind. It almost didn't seem real. Laura was such a nice girl that it didn't seem possible that her mom could be looking at me like that, especially when I was her daughter's boyfriend! I mean, if I'd been some delivery boy or something, it wouldn't have been quite so unexpected. Things like that did happen after all. I wasn't a delivery boy however and what was going on was downright shocking. What kind of mother would ogle her daughter's boyfriend? I wondered if she'd done this kind of thing before.

As I was telling her about the dance Laura and I attended, Katie put her hand on my knee. It was an innocent enough move in itself, but she kept it there longer than she should have. There really wasn't that much to it, she just touched my knee for a few moments, then drew her hand back and ran it through her hair. It probably wasn't anything more than it appeared, but after the way she'd been checking me out, it seemed rather significant. I half expected her to run her hand up my leg and grope me.

I had the distinct feeling I was being seduced. If the two of us had been alone in the house, I really think Laura's mom would have seriously put the moves on me. Part of me thought that was just ridiculous, but the rest of me knew it was true. Yet again, I found myself in a position that most boys would have found arousing, but that I found frightening. I mean, Katie was pretty hot for her age and I bet a lot of boys my age would have laid her in a second if they got the chance. Maybe not if they were dating Laura, but you know what I mean.

Finally, Laura came down the stairs and we beat a hasty retreat. I could practically feel her mom's eyes on my ass as we left. I don't think I'd been in such an awkward situation before in my entire life, and in the recent past I'd been in some pretty difficult and uncomfortable circumstances. I didn't feel violated or anything, just weird. After all, Katie had done no more than look at me and touch me on the knee. She hadn't come on to me. She hadn't touched me anywhere she shouldn't. She hadn't said anything inappropriate. Still, the whole thing was quite bizarre. I intended to spend as little time alone with Laura's mom as I could manage. I didn't need any more complications in my life. I already had a fake girlfriend. I didn't need my fake girlfriend's mother trying to seduce me. When did my life become a soap opera?

I drove Laura to Stephanie's house and we picked up Steph and Taylor there. We had to wait on Steph a few minutes too, but it wasn't nearly as bad as waiting on Laura. What an understatement! Tay looked pretty relieved when we walked in. I had the feeling Steph's father had been grilling him. What was it with parents? As bad as Tay's ordeal had been, I would have gladly traded him. An interrogation would be a lot easier to deal with than what I'd just been through.

Finally, we got out of there and made it to the theater. The previews were already on when we walked in. We would have been there in plenty of time, if we didn't have to wait on the girls. Why couldn't they be ready on time? That's another thing I liked about guys, they were always ready. No one ever had to wait on a guy while he fixed his hair or changed outfits. I wondered how my friends could stand dating girls. It was such a chore.

Of course, not all girls were like that. The female tendency to be late was a stereotype and I hated stereotypes, mainly because most of them were such crap. They were dangerous too and easy to believe. Not many people knew better than I what a stack of shit most stereotypes were and it was still easy for me to believe them sometimes. Laura and Steph were late, so I immediately bought into the "girls are always late" stereotype. No wonder others fell for them so easily. I just wished Laura and Steph didn't fit that particular stereotype. Why couldn't Tay and I have hooked up with girls who could be on time!

It was so dark I couldn't see a thing in the theater. Finally, my eyes adjusted enough that I could find us some seats without the risk of sitting on someone. We ended up sitting near the back: Steph, Tay, me, and Laura. I was happy about the seating arrangement. I wanted to be near Taylor. I just knew the girls would sit in the middle and I'd be separated from Tay, but it didn't happen. When the picture started, I put my arm around Laura, then pretty much ignored her. I did give her a little squeeze now and then, but my mind was elsewhere. I get pretty wrapped up in movies, especially if there's enough action, but Taylor was what really drew my attention away from Laura. She didn't seem to mind, or even notice. One thing I'd learned about Laura was that she was a major movie buff. She watched everything. I bet there wasn't a tape she hadn't rented at the video rental place. I was thrilled she was so into the picture, that way I could steal a few looks at Tay without her wondering what the hell was going on. My arm around her seemed to keep her content.

I wished that Taylor and I were alone. I couldn't help but think of Steph and Laura as unwanted intruders. In my mind I was on a date with Tay and we were saddled with two girls. It sucked. I had to keep thinking about saying all the right things to Laura. I had to concentrate on doing all the right things as well. Dating a girl was a lot of work. I wanted to make sure Laura had a good time, but with Taylor there, my mind wasn't really on my "girl". I wished for the hundredth time that Tay and I could be open about our relationship. Why couldn't I put my arm around him the way I did Laura? Sure, I could do it, but there would be hell to pay. A guy could put his arm around a girl without anyone thinking a thing about it. He could even make out with her. If I tried anything like that with Taylor we'd both get our asses kicked in the parking lot and be forever marked as perverts. Life wasn't fair. I wished we didn't have to sneak around like we were doing something wrong, when there wasn't a damn thing wrong with what we were doing. Why did everything have to be so hard?

I was keenly aware of Taylor beside me. Even when I was really into the picture, I could still feel his presence. I was aware of his every movement. I could catch the scent of his cologne and sometimes hear his breath. I was attuned to all those little things that most people ignore. Taylor's arm was on the arm rest between us. I stretched out my forearm against his. That mere touch was more exciting than anything that was going on up on the screen. Tay pressed his forearm against mine. I reached out and interlaced my fingers with his. Holding his hand filled me with a contentment and warmth that is hard to describe. It was one of those things that I wished I could keep doing forever and ever. If I could have, I would have frozen time and just sat there holding Taylor's hand for all eternity.

It was so dark in there no one could tell what we were doing. Laura or Steph could have noticed, but they were both too wrapped up in the film. The slight risk of discovery made it exciting. Tay and I knew well how danger heightened such experiences. We didn't seek out risk, but sometimes we had to take it. I'd given Tay a quick hug now and then, when one of our friends was just around the corner. Taylor had kissed me a time or two when his parents were in the next room and could have walked in at any second. We didn't do such things often and took pains to avoid discovery, but the possibility of discovery made what we were doing that much more intense.

When I touched Taylor, it wasn't merely a physical sensation. I felt as if I were touching his soul. Whenever we made that connection, I felt like the two of us were one. That was when I was the most content, when I was with Taylor. I felt like we were meant to be together. I felt that we were meant to be together forever.

Taylor and I held hands for the rest of the movie. I had my arm around Laura and Tay had his around Steph. To all the world we looked like any other boys with their girls. No one suspected what was really going on. No one guessed at our true nature. Yet again I felt like a vampire; powerful and vulnerable, an extraordinary creature walking among mere mortals. Taylor and I mingled among ordinary souls, living with the constant excitement and fear of discovery, and destruction. Each moment could be our last, and was therefore to be savored.

I had a wonderful time and all because I was able to hold Taylor's hand. Nothing else mattered. Laura, Steph, the movie, and all of those around us were without meaning, without consequence. They bore no importance in my life, left no imprint upon my existence. My whole world was the joy of holding Taylor's hand. Who would have thought that something so simple could bring so much pleasure?

The four of us lingered in the lobby after the movie. A lot of the guys from school were there, along with their dates. I talked to some of them a little, not much, but enough to make sure they saw me there with Laura. Taylor and I both tried to be very high profile when we were with our "girlfriends". Being seen dating a girl gave us the protection from suspicion we so desperately needed. No one suspects a vampire who can walk in the light of day.

It was too bad we couldn't have just taken Laura and Steph out now and then and be done with it. All that really mattered was being seen with girls in public. I wished we could have hired a couple of actresses to play the parts of our girl-friends. That would have made everything so much easier. We could have made a few appearances at dances, at movies, at ball games, and that would have been that. Unfortunately our "girls" weren't actresses, they were the real thing. We had to deal with the entire boyfriend-girlfriend relationship. It was far more time consuming than I'd ever dreamed. It involved a thousand details, all confusing, some bewildering, many exasperating. It was tough, but if it meant that Tay and I could avoid being outed, then it was all worth it.

8 Alone at Last

The first real chance Taylor and I had to be alone together came at an away soccer game. We were playing the Vikings, one of our toughest opponents. I always looked forward to playing the Vikings. It was usually a real challenge. This away game was so far away that the school sprung for a hotel. Not a very good hotel mind you, but it was far away from our girls. That in itself was a pretty attractive feature. For one evening at least, we were free! Tay and I convinced coach to switch our room assignments so we could share a room. It wasn't hard to talk him into it. We scored a lot of goals, so coach pretty much let us have our way. Like I said before, coach was pretty obsessed with winning.

Taylor and I sat together on the way to the game. We were surrounded by team-mates and couldn't talk about that night, but it was clear we were both thinking about it. Hell, it was all I could think about. I'd been thinking about it all day. I'd been thinking about it for days. I'd been thinking about it all my life.

I was excited, in more ways than one. I was also so nervous my stomach ached. That seemed to be happening to me a lot. I guess it was a sign that my life had become interesting. Other parts of my anatomy were aching as well, but for whole other reasons. Taylor and I hadn't discussed it, but I think we both knew what was going to happen when we were alone at last. I sure hoped he was thinking the same thoughts I was. Even if he wasn't, just being alone with him would be wonderful.

Every once in a while Taylor smiled at me and raised his eyebrows. I smiled back. It was the only way we had of communicating our feelings. We spent most of our time talking about the upcoming game. I was a soccer freak, and so was Tay, so talking soccer for hours on our way there was pretty cool. I just wished we could talk about a few other topics. It wasn't that there was all that much to say on those topics, but since we never seemed to be able to talk about certain things, the desire to do so was always on my mind.

It was a long trip. My butt was asleep by the time we got there. It felt good just to stand up and stretch. I was so filled with energy I was ready to explode. The entire team piled out of the bus screaming and hooting. I lead the charge.

"Let's kick some ass!" I yelled.

"Yeah!"

As we changed in the unfamiliar locker room, I felt like a gladiator getting ready to do battle. I almost felt sorry for our opponents. I was in the mood to kick ass and I was just the guy to do it. I watched as Taylor pulled off his shirt and slipped into his soccer jersey. Taylor was beautiful, he was a work of art. How could anyone not find him attractive?

I tore my eyes away from Taylor and thought about the game for a moment. The Vikings were tough as nails, but I knew if we could score soon enough, it would shake them up. If we couldn't score fast, we could still win, but it would be quite a struggle. That was okay too, soccer was my kind of fight. I thought of each game like a battle, a battle I intended to win. I think coach thought of it that way too, but he took things far too seriously. I wanted to win so bad I could taste it, but coach took it much farther. His attitude was "Come back with a win, or don't come back." Sometimes I think he lived his life vicariously through his players.

I slapped Tay on the back as we ran out of the locker room and onto the field. He smiled at me. He loved the struggle of the game as much as I did. We both loved the exertion, the sweat, the tactical maneuvers, the swift, split-second timing, the raw strength, the ancient male against male competition. There was something powerful and even erotic about the struggle to win, something primeval, almost sensual. I think I felt the most alive when I was fighting for a win. The more desperate the fight, the more intense the feeling. Even losing didn't diminish the feeling. All that really mattered was the struggle itself.

I was pumped. Soccer always got me pumped, but thinking about what might be happening after the game gave me a surge of adrenaline like I'd never had before. I was champing at the bit as the whistle blew. I kicked the ball forward and charged after it. I was like a freight train ready to plow down anyone who got in my way. I was so wild, I was nearly out of control. My eyes were practically bugging out of my head. If I was a lineman in a football game, I bet I would have scared the shit out of the guy across from me. I think a few of my opponents were a little leery of me, even though soccer isn't supposed to be a contact sport. It can be if you do it just right, but technically it's not.

Despite my excitement, or perhaps because of it, I had trouble keeping my mind on the game. It was hard to think about soccer instead of Taylor, especially since he was by my side. The mere sight of him sent my mind spinning in directions that had nothing to do with the game. His flowing blonde hair, handsome face, and lithe, firm body almost made me forget where I was. Such a distraction was new to me, but I made it part of the fight. It was but another opponent that I had to parry, dodge, and out maneuver.

We played well together, as always. Tay was pretty hyped up too. He was a mass of raw power, strength, and incredible skill. We were a terror on the field. Our team-mates, and coach, cheered us on. Soccer was the one thing at which both Taylor and I excelled. The field was ours.

The soccer game was a tough one and I nearly got kicked out. Some dude with an attitude on the other team was talking shit and pushing me around. I don't take crap off of anybody. I knocked his ass flat. I was smart enough to do it legally while he had the ball. I made it look like I was going after the ball and just couldn't stop. The referees bought it, but smart ass knew I'd plowed into him on purpose. I didn't care. I wanted him to know. He was pissed and started to come after me. I was ready, but the ref warned him off. We glared at each other for the rest of the game, but he didn't try anything. If he had started something, I would have kicked his ass. I'm not someone to mess with! I was so pumped I felt like I could take on him and his entire team. I must admit, I was a little sorry he didn't start a fight. My fist would have felt so good smashing into his punk face.

Taylor and I cut through the Viking's defense like it wasn't even there. I felt like I was unstoppable. I charged down the field, dribbling the ball around opponents, the wind racing through my hair. Whenever I got into a tight spot, Tay was there. I passed and Taylor ripped onward toward the goal. We scored less than two minutes into the game. That really shook our opponents up, just like I knew it would. We had them by the balls and I intended to squeeze.

It didn't take the Vikings long to adjust their defense. Taylor and I were clearly the ones to watch. That slowed us down, but gave the rest of our team a chance. The Vikings couldn't watch us all. The more they focused on me and

Tay, the more Brandon, Devon, and others slipped through. We were a team. It didn't matter who scored, as long as someone scored.

The Vikings were really tough on offense and broke through our defense several times. They didn't seem to be able to make a goal however. Our goalie made some kick ass saves and a few others came up with nice blocks too. If those guys hadn't been there, we would have been toast.

We ended up winning 7-1. We'd never done so well against the Vikings before. Tay and I scored two goals each so we were high on everybody's list. My back was getting sore from so many guys slapping it. I was going nuts. I just kept screaming "Yeah!" at the top of my lungs. I directed one "Yeah!" right at the punk who had been talking shit. He started to come after me again, but his buddies pulled him away. Too bad, that guy needed his ass kicked.

We stopped by a burger place after the game. I wolfed down two double cheeseburgers, a large order of fries, and a large drink. It was a wonder I wasn't fat, but I guess I just burned it all off. I was always lean. I wasn't the only one who was starving. Tay ate almost as much. So did Devon and Jon, who were sitting with us. Jon was one of my best buds on the team. He had hair as black as coal and an incredible build. I never thought of him as anything but a friend however. In fact, he was more like a brother. Devon and I were really tight too. It was great having close friends like that. Those guys meant a lot to me.

A couple of cute girls were staring at Taylor and I. We smiled at them and pretty soon they came over and started flirting with us big time. Girls just could not be encouraged at all. We just smiled at them to be nice and then there they were, practically drooling on us. We talked to the girls, but didn't do anything to encourage them. Gee, wouldn't the girls ever leave us alone? I had to admit, they were cute, but they were girls!

Tay and I could have been in a tight spot, but our "girlfriends" rescued us even though they weren't there. A thought crossed my mind. Maybe I could get them off us and do Devon and Jon both a favor. I smiled sweetly at the girl who had singled me out. I racked my brain trying to think of something really nice to say to her. A compliment can be disarming and I didn't want her all pissed when I tried to pass her off to my buddies.

"You have beautiful eyes, uhm.." I hesitated, I didn't even know her name.

"Shannon." she said. I could tell she was eating up my compliment. Girls always seemed to go for that crap. I wasn't lying however, she did have beautiful eyes. I still felt pretty corny saying it to her. I felt like I was quoting from a really bad novel. I had little choice however. I just couldn't think of anything better to say.

"Shannon." I repeated, smiling. "You have eyes just like my girlfriend." I looked at her apologetically.

That brought a frown to her face. She looked more than a little disappointed. Her friend quickly looked at Tay.

"I have a girlfriend too." Taylor said wistfully. Anyone watching would have really thought Tay was sorry he wasn't free to do something with that girl. The boy was a good actor.

Both Devon and Jon sat up a little straighter. They were smart enough not to say anything, but they looked like starving dogs drooling over a juicy steak.

"These two are free however." I said, indicating Jon and Devon. "If you don't mind ugly."

"Hey!" yelled Jon.

The girls laughed. I could tell by the way they looked at Jon and Devon that they thought they were anything but ugly.

"Maybe…" I suggested, arching my eyebrows and tilting my head towards my buddies.

Your average girl would probably have been insulted by being passed on to another guy, but these weren't average girls. I don't like to label anyone, but if I had to put a label on them, I would have called them sluts. It was pretty obvious what they were after. They were a teen-aged boy's dream come true.

The girls seemed intrigued by the idea. Devon and Jon were both pretty cute and I could see why girls would go for them. Since Tay and I were unavailable (they had no idea how unavailable) I guess the girls thought our buddies would suit their needs. I wasn't sure just what those needs were, but I knew what Devon and Jon were fantasizing about as they sat there. I had the feeling their fantasies weren't far removed from reality with those two girls. I had the feeling they'd be willing to do about anything, with anyone. Devon and Jon were sure interested in the girls. They were trying to be cool, but their eagerness was hard to hide. It was kind of funny. Their eyes were glazed over with lust and I bet neither one of them could have stood up just then if you know what I mean.

"Here, take our seats." I said, getting up and clearing my stuff out of the way. Taylor got up too and wandered off for some ice cream. I gave Devon and Jon a "you owe me one" smile as we left. I had the feeling those boys would be having a whole lot of fun, if they could sneak the girls into their hotel room.

Taylor handed me an ice cream cone and we walked over to the hotel to find coach and get our room key. We were alone for the first time that day, but we were both too shy to say much about what we both knew was going to happen. I felt light headed, almost giddy.

"I'm really looking forward to tonight." I said. It was as specific as I could get. I wanted to say more, but the words just wouldn't come. I felt stupid for being so awkward and shy. I was so happy I didn't care however. I felt like I could walk on air.

"Me too." said Taylor smiling. He was always smiling. That's one of the many things I loved about him. I could read all sorts of things in his smile just then. It was sweet, caring, mischievous, sensual, and just a touch wicked. The wicked part was particularly intriguing.

We found room 124, coaches room. He complimented us on the game, handed us our key, then went back to watching some program on cable. We were in room 214, one flight up. Our hotel was one of those with all the entrances to the rooms outside, not exactly the Ritz, but Tay and I didn't care. We climbed up the stairs. My legs were wobbly and my knees weak and it had nothing to do with the stairs or the soccer game we'd just played. I was nervous, but excited.

Taylor and I had no more than dropped our bags on the floor when a few of our team-mates dropped by. I wasn't interested in hosting the party room for the night. I wanted privacy. I could tell by the look on Taylor's face that he shared my feelings completely. We resigned ourselves to giving up a little of our time alone. Spending time with the guys was great, but it wasn't really what we wanted just then. Still, we couldn't exactly ask them to leave without arousing suspicion.

It seemed to take forever to get our team-mates to clear out of our room. We didn't want to be rude, but we wanted to be alone. Tay and I feigned exhaustion and they finally left. It was a moment we'd both been waiting for. When it came down to it however, I was so nervous I was actually trembling. It had started on the stairs, eased up a bit when our buddies were there, then returned with a vengeance when the last of our team-mates departed. My heart raced and I had a major case of butterflies in my stomach, yet again.

Tay sat on the edge of one bed, while I sat on the other. We silently gazed at each other. Both of us knew what we were thinking, but still it wasn't easy. We both sat there smiling shyly at each other. I felt distinctly stupid. I'd dreamed about having time alone with Taylor since we'd met. That moment had come and I was too shy to even speak. I wasn't the same boy who went wild on the soccer field or the same boy who nearly decked an opponent. What was the matter with me? Why was being with Tay so difficult?

I gazed at Tay. He was exceptionally good looking anytime, but his shyness made him cuter than ever. Taylor was still in his soccer uniform, as was I. That blue and white uniform made him particularly appealing. My eyes wandered slowly down his torso to his bare, muscular legs. Just looking at him made me feel all warm inside. Tay was beautifully built, a boy anyone could find appealing. My gaze roamed over his well shaped form and rested finally on his eyes. Tay smiled at me with a knowing, loving look and patted the bed beside him.

My heart was pounding in my chest as I arose, then seated myself next to him. Taylor was the boy of my dreams. I didn't feel I deserved him. It all seemed too good to possibly be true. I silently prayed that it was not all some sort of dream. If I awakened to find there was no Taylor in my life, I would not have wanted to live a moment longer.

I looked at Taylor timidly. I was almost afraid to touch him. I knew that I had to make the moves however. Tay was far more shy than I. At the moment, I wondered if that was possible, I felt like the shyest boy in the entire world. Why did I feel that way? I had held Taylor in my arms before, I had kissed him, but somehow it was different, it had far more meaning. Both of us knew what we wanted, but we were both too afraid to make the first move. I summoned all my courage and drew in a deep breath.

Slowly, almost hesitantly, I reached out to Taylor and to the life I knew could at last be mine. I gently guided him to his feet and we stood facing each other, mere inches apart. I wrapped my arms around his slim waist and drew him close. I hugged him tight. I felt secure in his embrace, and loved as I never had been before. His love flowed through me like a physical force. I can't begin to describe it. Even a poet could toil a lifetime and not be able to accurately relate the pure bliss that comes from being loved. Loving another is a wonderful thing, but being loved by another is the most extraordinary feeling in all the world.

Taylor felt so good in my arms, his firm body pressed against my own. I could feel his heartbeat, feel his sweet, hot breath on my neck, feel his warmth. I nuzzled my nose in his hair, drinking in his scent. It intoxicated me like wine.

I cared about Tay so much my heart ached. I was so happy to be with him it almost hurt. I wanted to protect him, help him, make him happy every day of his life. I wanted to hold him forever in my arms and never let him go.

We loosened our grip just enough so that we could gaze into each other's eyes. Our noses were barely an inch apart. I felt as if Tay was gazing into my very soul. I wanted to draw him in, make him a part of me. I wanted him to feel the depth of my love for him. I wanted him to understand just how much he meant to me. I wanted the two of us to be one. He nudged forward and rubbed his nose on mine.

I could feel his sweet breath upon me. We nudged forward hesitantly, awkwardly, until our lips met. Our kiss was gentle, halting, our lips barely brushing each other. As our hunger deepened, we kissed more forcefully, yet gently still. Our lips parted and our tongues entwined, Taylor's kiss was warm and pure.

We parted for a moment, smiles turning up the edges of our mouths. Taylor nuzzled my nose with his and kissed me again. I wrapped my arms more tightly around him and held him close as our lips and tongues explored. I had waited a painful eternity for this moment, and this moment alone was worth it all. Had I died just then, I would have died content.

Our paced quickened, our hearts raced. Taylor sought out my ear-lobes with his lips, sending me into an ecstasy of which I had only dreamed. We necked passionately, holding each other tight, and then our hands began to explore. Taylor's body was so strong, so firm. His movements were soft, gentle. His manner seemed a such a contrast to his form. His merest touch set me aflame with passion. He awakened my desire in a way no one else ever could. It didn't matter what I was doing with Tay, just so I was with him. I was in love.

My passion made me bold, more like my true self. I pulled Tay's shirt over his head and ran my hands over his beautiful torso. He was so smooth and firm. Touching him excited me beyond what I had previously thought possible. Everything with Taylor was new and exhilarating. I felt alive as I never had before. I pulled him to me and kissed him again, running my hands through his beautiful long blonde hair. Everything about Taylor was filled with beauty.

We explored each other, each touch, each caress a delight. In minutes, all our clothes lay in a pile on the floor. We sank onto Taylor's bed and made love, two virgins leading each other through a new and sensual world of pure delight. Our love was unhurried, but intense beyond imagination. No flame of passion ever burned as hot or as bright.

I experienced things that night I never had before. It was all just as wonderful and beautiful as I had dreamed and it was all because of Taylor. I loved him with all my heart and all that we did together was an expression of our love. Our hearts pounded in our chests, our breath came in gasps, Taylor and I sweat with exertion and still we kept making love. The hours passed and still we caressed and explored one another. We didn't pause until far into the night, morning real-ly, for the dim blue light was beginning to creep through the closed drapes.

When we grew still at last, I nuzzled up against Tay, feeling his warm skin against my own. I rested my head on his smooth, strong chest, listening to the rhythm of his heart, listening to his life. I fell asleep in his embrace and slept as I never had before.

We were awakened a scant few hours later by coach pounding on our door. We jumped out of bed and quickly dressed. We packed up and headed out, paus-ing to hold each other close and kiss once more. I was filled with contentment. Tay and I had done things during the night that I had only dreamed about before. All of it was so much more than I had imagined, because I was with someone I truly loved. I felt closer to Taylor and more in love with him than ever before.

We raced out the door, taking a moment to mess up my untouched bed. It was a long ride home and I was tired, but Tay was at my side. As long as he was there, I felt like I could conquer the world. We even managed to hold hands a little on the way home. Could life get any better?

9 A Confrontation at the Beach

"Miss me?" asked Laura as she hugged me tightly Monday morning at school.

"Of course!" I lied. Truthfully, I hadn't missed her at all. My mind had been filled with Tay and all we had experienced with each other. I was walking around in a blissful daze. Laura was an intrusion on my world. I wanted Taylor, not her. I wanted to hold hands in the halls with him, hug him, and kiss him, not Laura. If only I could let the world know he was my boyfriend, the way the world thought Laura was my girlfriend. That just could not be however. Sometimes I hated being a vampire, but it was my true nature. No, I didn't hate what I was, I hated how the world forced me to hide my true self. I was forced to suffer because others couldn't deal with what I was. There was nothing wrong with me, there was something wrong with those who would not, or could not, understand.

It was amazing how easy it was to lie once I got started. My first lies to Laura stuck in my throat like a ball of barbed wire, but soon I grew accustomed to the idea. I still didn't like it, but it was a necessary evil. Each lie was a little less difficult than the one before.

The lies were easier to handle, the guilt was not. I did everything I could to make it up to Laura. I tried my hardest to make her happy. I even spent time with her when I really wanted to be with Taylor. I knew in my heart that what I was doing was wrong, so I did all I could to make up for it and ease my conscience. No matter what I did however, my conscience would not let up. I felt that I should tell Laura the truth, but there was no way to do that without hurting her. It was too late. I was trapped.

I spoke with Taylor about my feelings over the whole girlfriend affair on a rare evening after practice when neither of us had to be with our girls. We sat in Taylor's living room and spoke softly so that his mother in the distant kitchen wouldn't hear.

"Mark, I know exactly how you feel. Even worse, this whole thing was my idea remember? Every time I think about how I'm lying to Steph, I feel like a major dick. I know it's wrong, but what can we do?"

I shrugged my shoulders. Knowing that Taylor felt as guilty as I over this whole affair made me love him all the more. A lot of guys can just use someone without giving it a thought, and they're not nearly so nice about it as Tay and I were. Neither of us were the kind of person who could do that however. I didn't want to be that kind of person. The guilt was painful and haunted me like a ghost, but I'd rather have felt the pain and guilt than no remorse at all. I did not want a heart of ice.

"I really feel like a piece of shit Taylor. The way Laura looks at me, the way she lights up whenever she sees me. She's really in love with me. I don't want to hurt her."

"I know. Steph's so happy whenever I'm around. She's even been talking about having sex with me. She said that she's never went farther with a boy than necking, but I was special, I was the one." Taylor paused, he looked like he was ready to cry. "I, I don't think I can do this anymore Mark. I know that the whole thing was my idea, but I don't think I can go on lying to Steph much longer. I can't bear to hurt her like this." Tears were welling up in Tay's eyes. He was truly a kind soul.

"I know." I said with genuine empathy. "But we can't just break up with them for no reason."

We sat in silence, there seemed to be no answer to our problem. We were in way over our heads, and we both knew it.

The weekend after our incredible night together, Taylor and I took our "girls" to a cookout/beach party at Koontz Lake. It was a little late in the year for swimming, but the temperature had been above normal for weeks. It was a bright sunny day too. It was everyone's last chance to swim and enjoy the sun before it got too cold.

Brandon had invited us earlier in the week. A bunch of the guys from the team were coming, as well as a few others, plus all the girlfriends, so it was a pretty big crowd. We arrived a little after noon, lugging three huge coolers stuffed with soft drinks. Everyone was bringing something and we were in charge of beverages. I know most of the guys would have preferred beer, but the lake area was highly patrolled and besides, it wouldn't exactly have been easy to get our hands on alcohol.

Brandon was already flipping burgers on a grill when we got there. There were mounds of food spread out all over picnic tables. There were a ton of kids there, playing Frisbee, football, and just messing around.

Tay and I wasted no time. We pulled off our shirts, shoes, and socks and dove into the lake. The water was pretty warm and the sun downright hot. Laura and Steph weren't far behind us. I have to admit that they both looked pretty good in their skimpy swim-suits. I saw a lot of guys eyeing them and my chest swelled a little with pride over having such a pretty girl, even if she wasn't really my girl-friend. There was just something about having what other guys wanted.

Taylor and I wrestled around in the water with some of the other guys. The girls mainly just floated around. Some of the guys there looked pretty hot. Devon and Jon in particular had really nice builds. I stole a few glances of them now and then. I caught Tay looking at them too. He smiled at me and arched his eyebrows. It was cool being with someone who appreciated the beauty of the male form.

I wasn't jealous that Tay was looking at other guys. I knew that's all he was doing, looking. Taylor was just like me, he took commitment seriously. We were boyfriends and neither of us would consider going with anyone else. There was no need for jealousy. It was great that we could trust each other like that.

Laura and Steph didn't swim long. They sunned themselves on the shore while Taylor and I horsed around with the guys. They were busy talking to each other, so they didn't mind that we weren't right there with them.

I looked over and noticed a couple of Seniors were flirting with Laura. One of them, Steve, was obviously putting the moves on her. I didn't really care of course, but I had to look like I did. Steve was a major wrestling stud, on the varsity team and was accustomed to having about any girl he wanted. I could see why, he was hot as hell. He was really built, with muscles bulging out everywhere. If that wasn't enough, he was one of the most attractive guys at school, with jet black hair and steely blue eyes that made all the girls swoon. To be honest, he had a pretty pronounced effect on me too. He was gorgeous. Before Tay came along, I'd spent a lot of time thinking about Steve.

I was seeing him in an entirely different light as he put the moves on my girl. He knew she was going with me. Hell, everyone knew it. I thought for a moment that I'd found a way out of the mess I'd gotten myself into. If I let him steal her away, I wouldn't have to worry about her anymore. I couldn't do that however. It would make me look like a wimp and everyone would wonder why I didn't do anything. It would probably cause suspicions to rise and I'd be right where I was before Tay and I took up our "girlfriends". Besides, I didn't take shit off anyone, and Steve making a play for my girl right in front of me was shit.

I stepped out of the water and walked toward Steve. I couldn't believe what he was doing, and right in front of all my friends! It was an outright challenge. I wondered what the fuck he thought he was pulling. Despite the fact that I didn't really want Laura, what he was doing pissed me off. The closer I got, the madder I became. I think the crowd realized it too. I could see a lot of them watching me as I approached. I was hot. Instead of talking, I walked up to Steve and shoved him away from Laura. I know I was acting like Neanderthal Man, but once I got pissed, I started losing control.

"Back off fucker!" yelled Steve.

"You back off!" I yelled right back.

A crowd gathered around us. They were waiting for a fight and were likely to get one. I was too bull headed to back away and Steve wasn't likely to back off either. We were both jocks with reputations to protect.

Backing off would have been the smart move for me. Those bulging muscles of Steve's weren't just for looks. I was pretty strong, but he was undoubtedly stronger. He had a good three inches on me in height and probably weighed twenty or thirty pounds more, all of it muscle. He was a top-notch wrestler too, something I knew next to nothing about. I would quite likely get my ass kicked if we tangled, but I wasn't about to back down.

I could feel Tay standing behind me, but he didn't interfere. He knew it was my fight and that I wouldn't want him to step in. We seemed to instinctively know what the other was thinking.

Steve was pretty intimidating. He wasn't wearing a shirt and the muscles of his torso flexed with his slightest movement. His bulging biceps were a sign of just how hard he could punch. If I had any sense at all, I would have gotten the hell out there. I was pissed however. I wasn't backing down.

We just stood there, glaring at each other. Steve probably stared a lot of guys down. He probably awed them with his strength. Not me.

"Bring it on Mark." he said, motioning me toward him with his fingers. "Come on Mark and I'll kick your ass."

That was it. I was going to fuck him up bad, or get beat senseless trying. I growled and flew into him, my fist smashing into his jaw before he even saw it coming. I punched him again, this time in the stomach, before he knocked me up side the head. That dazed me a little, but I jammed my fist into his face again. His head snapped back and I landed a quick right.

Steve was tough. He took the pain and just kept coming at me. Our fists flew. Steve got me in the left eye. I knew I'd have a black eye in the morning. He also smashed me in the face with a powerful right and busted my lip. I swear it loosened my teeth. He punched me hard in the stomach and I doubled over. I returned the favor, my fist contacting with his hard abs with a satisfying thump.

Steve rushed me and slammed me to the ground. We rolled around on the sand, fists flailing, beating the shit out of each other. Steve let loose a small, derisive laugh and smirked at me. I flew into a rage. I was totally out of control. I tore into him, punching him so fast he didn't have time to recover. In seconds he was on his back and I was on top of him, pounding him. I rammed my fist into his face, his chest, his stomach. I went wild. Steve stopped trying to hit me and tried to protect himself from the blows. I was all over him. I was in such a rage I wanted to kill him. I hit him over and over until some of the guys pulled me off him. Even then, I fought to get at him. They held me back however until I calmed down a bit. Steve pulled himself to his feet and limped away. The guys holding me didn't let go until Steve's buddies had put him into a car and driven away.

"Mark, your lip." said Laura. She was all concerned.

"I'm okay." I said.

"You really kicked his ass." said Brandon.

I smiled. I guess I did kick his ass. I couldn't quite believe I'd managed it. By all rights he should have mopped up the beach with me. I guess I just got lucky. Either that or my out of control temper just overpowered his strength and determination. Either way, I didn't want to experience it again. My whole body hurt like hell.

The excitement was over and everyone went back to goofing around. I knew I'd be the talk of the school on Monday morning. Laura looked impressed and worried, so did Taylor. Tay was looking me over, making sure I wasn't more hurt than I appeared to be. Laura was fawning over me.

I must admit. I was kind of proud of myself. I know fighting shouldn't be the answer, but sometimes it is. Steve should have whipped my ass with ease, but I managed to take him. I was pleased with myself over that, and over the fact that

I hadn't backed down when I really thought he was going to beat the shit out of me.

A lot of the guys, and the girls, were impressed as well. I could tell by the way they looked at me and the comments they made. Jon led me off to the bath house to clean up, my busted lip had made a pretty nasty mess. It wasn't really all that bad however, it just looked terrible.

Jon couldn't resist talking to me about the fight as I cleaned the blood away.

"Way to go Mark!"

"Thanks."

"I'd wouldn't have put up with that either, not if he was messing with my girl. Well, if I had a girl that is!" he said laughing.

No one else could overhear us, so I asked him something that had been on my mind.

"You dated Laura before, didn't you?"

"Yeah, about a year ago. We weren't too compatible."

"What did you think about her mom?"

"Well, she was okay I guess, kind of pretty. Why?" Jon looked at me kind of confused.

"Did she ever... I mean, did she ever act... odd when you were around her?"

"What do you mean?"

I looked around to make sure we were alone, even though I knew we were.

"Promise me you won't tell anyone about this, anyone."

"Okay, I promise. What's the big deal?"

"Well, I'm not exactly sure, but I think Laura's mom wants me."

"What for? To mow her lawn?"

"You know what I mean!"

"No, I don't."

It was clear by the look on his face that he really didn't understand. I thought it was pretty damned obvious.

"I mean, she wants me. She wants my body."

"You are shitting me." Jon looked completely dumbfounded.

"No! I'm not even sure, but, well, I'm pretty sure."

"What did she do?"

I told Jon about the whole thing. It had really been bugging me. Just before we came to the lake I was alone with Katie for just a few minutes while I was waiting on Laura. She was practically undressing me with her eyes. My shoulders were real stiff and when I casually mentioned it she started rubbing them. Her hands even wandered down onto my chest. Luckily, Laura came into the room before her mom had time to do much and I made my getaway. It made me more suspicious than ever. Hell, the way she touched me pretty much removed all doubt.

"You dog you, Laura and her mother!" Jon whistled.

"It's not funny!"

He could tell I was kind of upset, so he stopped kidding around.

"It sounds to me like she wants you Mark. If you're not interested in older women, I'd stay clear of her."

"That's my plan. So she never came onto you, or looked you over or anything?" I asked.

"No. Well, she did look at me sometimes, but I think that's all she was doing. I don't think she was after me or anything. I guess I just don't have what you've got Mark."

"Thanks a lot." I said sarcastically.

"Gee, all the women want you Mark." Jon was half kidding, half serious.

"Yeah," I said, "it's a curse." Little did Jon know that I really thought of it that way.

"May I be cursed like that." he wished out loud. With his looks, I was sure his wish would come true.

My parents weren't too happy when I got home. I had to tell them the whole story of what happened. Dad didn't say so in front of mom, but I knew he was proud of me. I could tell by the way he looked at me. Mom took me into the emergency room and they stitched up my lip. It hurt like hell.

I went into school Monday morning with a black eye and stitches. I was right, everyone was talking how I kicked Steve's ass. I wished they hadn't made such a big deal out of it, although the attention was kind of cool.

I'd had time to cool down. I wasn't mad at Steve anymore. He'd been a real dick at the lake, but that was all over. I was ready to forget the whole thing. I wasn't so sure about Steve however. He'd gotten his ass kicked and I didn't know if he could swallow that or not. He might feel the need to prove to everyone that he could take me. I wasn't going to provoke him. My anger was gone and I didn't want to tangle with him again. I knew I was lucky at the lake. He should have beat the shit out of me, next time, he probably would. That's why I wished everyone would just stop talking about it. If everyone kept going on and on about how I kicked his ass, there was no way Steve could just let it go, he had a reputation to protect.

I thought we were going to tangle again at lunch. I was eating with Tay and some of the guys. Steve was sitting not too far away and I could tell he was fuming over having lost the fight. I was thankful that everyone was wise enough not to mention it. Unfortunately, everyone wasn't that wise. Randy, a dumb ass junior I hardly knew, had to open his big mouth.

"You really kicked Steve's ass all over the beach didn't you Mark?" he said.

I couldn't believe how stupid he was. There was no way Steve could ignore that remark. The whole table got real quiet. I could practically hear Steve's teeth grinding. I wanted to pound for Randy for being such a dip-shit. I knew I was seconds away from a fight. I tried my best to avoid it.

"I'd say we kicked each other's ass." I said. "Laura didn't give me this busted lip or black eye!" I was hoping to make peace with Steve. If I acted cocky, he'd have no choice but to take me down. If I acknowledged how tough he was, he might be able to let it go.

"I sure as hell don't want to tangle with him again." I said, looking straight at Steve. "He about took my head off." It was the truth and there was no shame in admitting it. My attitude had the desired effect. Steve looked at me, without anger in his eyes.

"You're sure tougher than you look." he said.

"Nah, not tougher, just pissed, and lucky as hell."

Steve actually laughed.

"Friends?" I asked.

"Friends." That was it. Everything was cool between me and Steve. Guys seemed to be able to settle things so much better than girls.

10 Gazing at the Stars

Taylor and I didn't have a chance to be alone together for days at a time. Our guilt forced us to spend time with our "girls" and do everything we could to make up for using them. We couldn't think of a way to disentangle ourselves from the web of deceit we'd woven, it's grip was just too strong. It seemed that the more we struggled against it, the tighter it's hold became. There was just no way out.

The one time that we could be together now and then was late at night, when we were both supposed to be home in bed. Neither of us lived too far away from the school, so we usually met at the soccer fields. Late at night, no one was around and we didn't have to worry much about being spotted. We always lay side by side looking up at the stars. The soccer field was dark and we had a clear view of the heavens. We lay there and talked about all the things we couldn't talk about around others. I loved laying there with Tay at my side, or better yet with Taylor in my arms. He liked it when I held him and I liked nothing better. I loved being close to him. Sometimes the nights were chill, but we kept each other warm.

"You know they say when you look at the stars, you're looking back in time." said Taylor.

"Really?" I asked. I'd never heard of such a thing before.

"Yeah, they're so far away that the light takes years and years to reach us, sometimes hundreds of years, sometimes thousands."

"That is really cool." I said, looking far above us into the sky.

"Take that star there." said Taylor, pointing to an especially bright star almost directly overhead. "What we're seeing now could be how that star looked thousands of years ago. Just think about it. We weren't even born yet, neither were our parents, nor theirs. Nothing that we know even existed yet."

Sometimes Taylor could get really deep. That's something I loved about him, the way he could get all deep and dreamy about something. I guess it was the poet in him. Taylor took my mind a lot of places it had never been before.

"Have you ever thought about telling your parents?" he asked.

I wasn't ready for the change of topic. I had to think about it for a moment.

"You mean about us? Or just about being attracted to guys?"

"Both."

"I've thought about it." I said. "But I don't think I could ever do it. I know they wouldn't understand."

"Same here." said Taylor. "I wish I could tell them all about you, about us. I wish they could understand and be happy for me, but I don't think they could."

"It hurts doesn't it." I said.

"Yes."

"You know," I said. "So many times I've wanted to tell my parents about you and about how much I love you, how happy I am when I'm with you. I really don't think they could handle it though. Mom would probably get all upset and wonder where she'd gone wrong. She'd be all worried about me getting aids or something like that. And Dad, he'd go nuts if he knew I was gay. I really think he'd hate me if he knew."

"Maybe not." said Taylor.

"Maybe not, but I think he would. He's always making comments about the "queers". He'd shit if he knew I was into guys."

We both grew silent. I drew Tay closer and held him as if I could protect him from all the dangers of the world. I knew I couldn't, but I wished that I could. Nothing was more important to me than Taylor.

We lay there watching the stars, looking through space and back into time. I wondered why so many people got so upset over homosexuals. It all seemed pretty silly to me. With all the problems in the world, why did loving a member of one's own sex have to be such a big deal? Most of the world's problems were created by overpopulation. It was the cause of shortages, poverty, plagues, and wars. It looked to me like people would be glad there were homosexuals. Just think of it, thousands and thousands of people who would never reproduce. It seemed to me that the world needed more people like that.

"I wonder why they hate us." I said out loud, almost without knowing I'd done so. Taylor looked at me, not quite certain what I meant. "You know, I wonder why so many people are down on gays."

"Because we're different." said Taylor. "We dare to go against what they believe, so they think we're dangerous or something."

"It looks like they'd have figured out by now that we aren't."

"Ah, most of them probably know it. They just won't admit to themselves that they know it. They need someone to blame things on."

"Yeah," I said, "I guess you're right." I was silent for a moment. "I wish we could go someplace where being gay or straight didn't matter, someplace with just people, you know, just people."

"Maybe someday we can find that place together." said Taylor.

I held him tight. Taylor turned to me and kissed me. I forgot all about the world and it's problems as we kissed each other on the soccer field.

11 A Fright in the Night

On Saturday night the varsity soccer team had an unofficial party in the grave-yard on the outskirts of town. The idea was basically to hide out and drink beer until we puked. It sounded like fun to me. A few guys not on the team were coming, but everyone on the team would be there. I picked Taylor up and drove out about ten. I pushed all thoughts of guilt out of my mind and determined to enjoy myself. I wasn't really that big on drinking, and neither was Tay, but I did enjoy a slight buzz. Besides, it was a chance to be with our soccer buddies, instead of our girls. Laura and Steph understood, it was a guy thing. Besides, it wouldn't hurt Taylor and I to work on our "regular guy" facade. Drinking with our friends would help us avoid suspicion. Everyone knew gay guys weren't into beer, what a joke.

We parked a good distance from the grave yard and walked the rest of the way. Everyone was supposed to do that. It wouldn't do to have a big bunch of cars parked by the cemetery, it would surely draw unwanted attention. I pulled back the heavy iron gate and it groaned in protest. The place looked deserted. The party was supposed to be deep into the grave yard however, just before the edge of the forest on the far side, to avoid detection. If we got caught, we'd be up shit creek. Some people had no tolerance for under-aged drinking.

I'm no coward, but the hairs on the back of my neck stood on end as we walked between the ancient, moss covered stones. Taylor took my hand and held it tight. I pulled him close, protecting him from the terrors of the dark. My own fears dissolved as I sought to comfort him. I was his protector. Besides, I teased myself, vampires shouldn't be afraid of the night. I didn't know why I was so jumpy in the first place. I guess I thought some moldering hand would reach out to grab me from the grave.

There was little light. What illumination the moon cast was dimmed by tattered clouds drifting overhead. I felt like I was in some horror movie. There was fear in Taylor's eyes, not great fear, but an edgy look. Being in a grave yard at night can be unsettling. I looked around to make sure no one was there and pulled Taylor close. I hugged him tight and kissed him. A noise close by scared the shit out of us both, more because we thought we'd been caught necking than because of any ghosts. Still, it was spooky out there.

We picked our way through the tombstones and mausoleums I was beginning to think that we'd been had. I was beginning to suspect that there was no party and the guys had just sent us into a grave yard at night for a joke. Just then I heard laughing in the distance. We followed the sound and in a few moments we found our buddies. The party was in full swing.

"Hey Tay!" said Brandon. He was already swaying a little.

"What up Mark?" asked Jon.

Devon tossed us each a beer and we sat in a circle with the other guys. A lantern cast a golden glow on our young faces. We laughed and talked, about soccer, football, girls, and mostly nothing at all. The more everyone drank, the more they laughed, and the more they talked about nothing. It didn't matter, everything was funny. It wasn't long at all before some of our team-mates were downright drunk. Devon climbed to the top of a large monument and perched there, claiming to be king of the grave yard. Greg turned on a radio and the old cemetery was filled with loud music.

"Turn it down dude!" yelled Devon. "You wanna wake em all up?" He gestured to the graves all around us and laughed, nearly falling off his perch.

Greg toned it down a bit. I shook my head. I was getting a nice buzz. I felt all warm and cozy and happy. I tried not to drink too much however. I didn't want to get wasted like the other guys. My parents would shit a brick if I came in drunk.

Taylor was a little far gone too, more so than me. He seemed to have even a lower tolerance for alcohol than I did and mine wasn't too great. I rarely drank and beer hit me pretty hard. I was smart enough to avoid the harder stuff that was being passed around, well, at least for the most part.

"You guys know," said Jon, "that old man Swensen bought it out here, right where we're sitting."

The guys grew quiet. Jon was getting ready to tell one of his scary tales. He had a reputation for that. Something about the sound of his voice, and the way he told a story, inspired terror in his listeners. He'd hardly started and the hair on the back of my neck was standing on end. Of course, being in the middle of a grave yard probably had something to do with that. No where was a ghost story more frightening than among the dead.

"They found him out here a few years ago, stiff as a board and white as a sheet."

"What happened?" asked Ethan.

"I gotta take a piss." said Taylor as he leaned over to me. I knew he was getting drunk. He was usually too shy to say anything like that. He pulled himself to his feet, holding onto my shoulder to keep from falling. He was a little unsteady. He walked off, balancing himself by gripping tomb stones as he went on his way.

Jon was continuing his tale. All eyes were on him, most of them wide with fear.

"They say he just died of a heart attack, but everyone knows that's not what happened. His wife is buried right over there." he said pointing to a grave some of the guys were near. "He was real mean to her when she was alive. They say he beat her. Anyway, I heard that he was walking through the grave yard half drunk, and when he walked past his wife's grave, a hand reached out and GRABBED HIM!" I flinched, even though I knew Jon was going to yell like that. In our current surroundings Jon's tale was far more frightening than it would have been otherwise.

"You about made me shit my pants!" said Ethan.

Jon smiled, and went on.

"She pulled herself out of her grave, holding onto his ankle. He screamed bloody murder, but there was no one living to hear him. She pulled him to the ground and climbed on top of him, her fetid stench making him sick, maggots falling from her face. Her bony, putrid fingers closed around his neck and she squeezed the life out of him as she kissed him with her rotting lips. When he was dead, she crawled back in her grave and they found him where she'd killed him, a few days later. They say she pulls herself from her grave whenever anyone disturbs it and strangles them with her rotting, putrid fingers."

Some of the guys sitting near the grave edged away, as if fearful she might reach out for them, even though they knew Jon was making the whole thing up.

Taylor still hadn't returned when Jon finished his story. I was beginning to get a little worried, maybe he was sick or something. I arose and dusted off the seat of my pants.

"I'll be back in a minute guys. I want to get out of here before Jon starts the inevitable 'hook on the car door' story."

"Oh, that's a good one." said Jon. "This young couple were out in the woods, getting it on…"

I slipped away as Jon spun his tale. I found Taylor not far distant, staring at a large tomb stone.

"Hey Mark. Look at this." he said, pointing to a small picture on the stone. "When you move, it's eyes follow you."

"Sure thing Taylor." I said. "Let's go back."

Taylor looked a little weird in his semi-inebriated state. He was just a little too relaxed, but hell so was I. Before I even realized what was happening, he grabbed me and kissed me. He started tugging at my shirt.

"Whoa Taylor." I said. "Not here."

Taylor nodded and let me lead him back to the party. He leaned up against a tomb stone and accepted another beer. I was getting afraid of what he might do. Drinking seemed to change him, make him more aggressive and outgoing. It wasn't Taylor that fucked up however, it was me.

I knew it was stupid, but I kept drinking. Everyone was doing it and it just seemed like the thing to do. I felt my inhibitions lower and along with it went my common sense. It was getting a little chilly and I snuggled up against Tay. Pretty soon I had my arm around him and was practically in his lap. I leaned over and whispered to him, my lips barely an inch from his ear. Taylor turned to face me and our lips brushed against each other. We didn't kiss, but gazed into each other's eyes. My hand wandered onto his leg. I was rubbing his thigh without even thinking about it.

"What are you fags doing?" yelled Devon.

I pulled away from Taylor in a flash. Devon was staring down at us. All I could think was "Oh fuck! I've done it now!"

"What is all the noise about?" asked Jon. Now everyone was looking in our direction.

"Mark and Taylor were all over each other, they're fags dude!"

Neither Taylor nor I said a word. We were fucked.

"You're drunk." said Jon, dismissing him.

Devon was a little unsteady on his feet. He had the distinct look of someone who was about to barf. He stood there, just staring at us.

"I still think they're fags."

"In the condition you're in, you wouldn't know a fag if he bit you!" yelled Brandon. He laughed so hard at his own joke he fell right off the tombstone he'd been sitting on.

"Bite me and we'll see!" said Devon. That got all the guys laughing.

It was time to go. I pulled Tay up and led him away from the party. We'd done enough damage for one night. I don't even remember taking Taylor home. I woke up the next morning with a bad head ache and a sense of panic in my gut.

I had little to worry about however. Devon didn't mention the incident at all on Monday at school. I don't know if he just didn't remember what happened (a distinct possibility) or if he just chalked it up to his drunken state. My memory was a little fuzzy too, but I knew I'd almost exposed myself, and Taylor, to our buddies. It was the only time I'd ever drank heavily and I'd almost ruined my life. I had narrowly avoided disaster. I wasn't about to make that mistake again.

After that one little incident everything was cool. Taylor and I even started to find a little time to spend together. Our "girlfriends" took up most of our time, but we managed at least one evening a week with each other, sometimes more. Occasionally we worked in some time on the weekends too, and, of course, we spent some late nights together on the soccer field watching the stars.

12 The Dream Becomes a Nightmare

Just when everything seemed to be going just right, my whole world collapsed. I was in heaven, then suddenly hell. It all started out well and innocently enough. Taylor came over to my house about ten on a warm Sunday morning. Mom even made us blueberry pancakes for breakfast. We sat at the kitchen table and ate and talked. I could tell mom really liked Taylor. Of course, what was not to like? Taylor was always polite and kind. Around my mom he was downright charming. I think she was about ready to adopt him! She was always going on about him when he wasn't there.

After breakfast Taylor and I went to my room. We messed around on the Internet for a while, mainly looking at soccer and music sites. After that we sat on my bed and listened to a few CD's. I gazed into Taylor's eyes. I was so in love with him.

I got up for a moment and latched my door. I turned back to Taylor and his eyes locked onto mine. I sat down by him again and drew him close. We hugged, then kissed. We sank back onto my bed and made out for about half an hour. There was nothing more wonderful than being with my Taylor.

"We'd better stop." I said, after we'd been going at it for a good, long time.

"You want to stop?" asked Taylor mischievously.

"No." I said smiling. "But we'd better anyway."

We both laughed and nuzzled our noses together. Being with Taylor made me so happy. Even better, being with me made Taylor happy.

After making out on my bed, we both needed to burn off some excess energy, so we grabbed a soccer ball and headed outside. My parents had a large back yard and years before had set up a soccer goal so I could practice. Tay and I took turns as goalie, while the other tried to score. Both of us did a lot of scoring, since neither of us was a very good goalie. I had trained myself so thoroughly not to use my hands that I was uncomfortable doing so to stop the ball. It didn't matter, we had fun.

It was really hot out there and soon we pulled off our shirts. That let Tay score on me even more. The sight of his bare chest, gleaming with sweat, distracted me more than I can describe. I couldn't keep my mind on the ball. I found myself gazing dreamily at his beautiful form.

"Mark!" my mom called me from the house.

"Just a sec Tay."

I ran up to the house, talked to mom, then quickly ran back to Taylor.

"My parents are going to the mall, then a movie. They asked if we wanted to come, but I told them we'd just stay here. That's okay isn't it? If it's not, we can still catch them."

"Yeah, I'd much better be alone with you."

Tay kicked the ball and it hurtled past me into the goal.

"Hey! That one doesn't count!" I yelled.

"But the next one will!"

I took up a defensive stance. I tried to focus on the ball, but all I could really concentrate on was Taylor's lithe form. After getting the ball past me several times Taylor smiled at me wickedly. He knew what was happening!

After that he intentionally distracted me and he knew just how to do it. I renewed my efforts to ignore him and just concentrate on stopping the ball, but it was no use. Tay was getting really cocky. He had a smirk on his face that just wouldn't go away. After he scored on me yet again he broke out in laughter.

I grabbed him and wrestled him to the ground. The physical contact with his firm, sweaty body made me yearn to be alone with him as we had been during our away game and a handful of times after that. I loved Taylor dearly, and being near him had a certain effect on me. I was still all worked up from making out with him earlier and I didn't seem to be able to calm back down. We broke off our wrestling match before things went too far and the neighbors began to wonder about us. My shorts were already a little tented.

Tay took the goal and I scored on him time after time. I wasn't the only one distracted. I enjoyed his predicament and the attention. It made me feel good about myself, knowing what was going through Taylor's mind as he looked at me.

After an hour we were both hot, sweaty, and more than a little smelly. Our bodies were covered with mud and grass stains, streaked by the streams of sweat running down our torsos. We went inside. We climbed the stairs to my room.

"I need a shower." said Taylor.

I looked at him and wrinkled my nose, "Yes."

"Hey, you aren't exactly smelling sweet either!"

I laughed.

"You can use my shower. There are towels in the closet. I'll use the one downstairs."

I'd rather have showered with Taylor, but I knew I had to maintain control. We were in my house, but it was also my parents house. He started undressing by my bed. I left before he drove me out of my mind with desire. I walked down stairs, stripped, and climbed into the shower. The hot water felt so good as it beat down upon me. Probably I should have been taking a cold shower, considering the way I was all heated up. I couldn't help but think of Taylor taking a shower just upstairs. That sure didn't help me cool down any! I was in love with him and the mere sight of him aroused me. Thinking about him naked in the shower, with hot, steaming water pounding down on his young, hard body was about more than I could take. My breath was coming fast and hard and my heart pounded away in my chest.

I lathered up my hair and ran the soapy washcloth all over my sweaty body. That didn't help me calm down either. It seemed that everything I did just aroused me more. I thought about just jerking off in the shower to get myself under control, but instead I just rinsed off quickly then dried myself with a towel.

I didn't want to put my sweaty, dirty clothes back on, so I just wrapped my towel around my waist and went back upstairs. I was rummaging through my dresser for something to wear when Tay stepped out of the bathroom. He was clad in nothing but a towel wrapped around his waist. His hair was wet and hung down perfectly straight, brushing his shoulders. I couldn't keep from running my eyes down his smooth, firm body. Doing so drove me out of my mind with desire. I loved him and I wanted him.

I forgot all about finding something to wear and stepped towards Tay. I pulled him toward me and kissed him. His lips tasted so sweet I wanted to devour him. I slid my tongue along his as we made love with our lips. I sighed with contentment and hugged him so hard I almost crushed him. I was totally, completely in love with him.

We were alone, the house was empty. We had started something that could not be stopped. Taylor pressed his hard, naked torso against mine. I could feel the muscles of his chest pressing into my own. Taylor was so beautiful, he was the very essence of young manhood.

I pressed my lips to his and kissed him passionately once more. It awoke within me a primal urge that could not be denied. I could have kissed Tay forever. I felt so safe, secure, and loved when I was in his arms. Our chests pressed hard against each other. I ran my hands down his back, and lower still. Tay's wet hair clung to his face and made him look cuter than ever. We necked ever more intensely and our towels fell to the floor. We pressed ourselves against each other, enjoying the closeness, intimacy, and hardness.

Our lips parted and I pulled Tay to my bed. We lay down upon it, our lips meeting once more. Our hands sought out each others body and we began to express our love with actions the way we did so often with words. Being with Tay was like a dream come true, more than that, Tay was my reason for living. Without him, I was lonely, miserable, an outsider to the world. With him I was loved, happy, and whole.

Our lovemaking was the most beautiful thing in the world. It wasn't just sex, it was far, far more. Only someone who deeply loves another could understand. All that we did was an expression of love for the other. And oh how I loved Tay. I held him so tight against me I nearly squeezed the life out of him. He returned my embrace with equal intensity. Knowing that his love for me equaled my own love was the most important thing in the universe.

Our hands and lips were everywhere. Our hearts pounded, our pulse quickened, our breath came hard and fast. A thin mist of perspiration covered our bodies. We moaned and whimpered in pure bliss. Tay and I were one. My entire body was an explosion of pure pleasure. Tay awakened feelings and sensations in me that I never thought possible. Our love making went beyond what it is possible to describe. We made love, over and over again. We were tireless young men, so involved with each other, so in love, that we could not stop.

It was all so beautiful, it was like a dream. I had never been so happy as I was at that moment.

My dream turned into a nightmare without a hint of warning. The door to my bedroom opened and my father entered. He didn't bother to knock, and I hadn't thought to lock the door. I've lamented my stupidity ceaselessly since that day.

"Mark, could you…. My God! What the fuck is going on in here?"

Tay and I were naked on my bed, in the middle of making love. There was no way to deny what was going on. Tay bolted for the bathroom, slammed and locked the door, crying "Oh fuck! Oh fuck!" and "Oh my God!" over and over. Tears ran down his face as he sought to escape from my father. He only just managed. My father nearly snagged him as he ran past. Only a quick dodge on Tay's part allowed him to evade my father's wrath.

I covered my nakedness with the sheets as my father screamed at me in rage.

"What do you think you're doing? How could you do this under my roof?" He was out of control. I'd never seen him that furious before. He turned and pounded on the bathroom door.

"Come out of there you little faggot! Come out of there right now!"

Taylor didn't make a sound. He wasn't about to come out of there. I wouldn't have either. If I could have ran, I would have. While dad was pounding on the door, I used the opportunity to pull on my boxers. When Tay wouldn't open up, dad turned back on me. There was murder in his eyes. I really thought my own father was going to kill me, really kill me, not just beat the crap out of me, kill me.

My mom ran into my room, wondering what all the noise was about.

"What's going on in here?" she asked, her face etched with concern.

"Why don't you ask your faggot son, or his faggot friend in the bathroom!"

I ran behind my mom. Dad tried to get around her to get at me, but she blocked his path. If I wasn't about to quite literally die, the scene would have been funny. My dad is a big man, about 6'4" and over 200 pounds. I was a 6' jock and weighed about 165, while my mom was this tiny little 5'6", 110 pound sprite of a woman. There I was, a tall, muscular soccer stud and I had to take refuge behind my tiny mom. She wasn't half the size of my dad, but she was holding her own. She held him back just by looking at him. It was lucky for me, she was the only thing protecting me from certain death.

"Jeffery calm down."

"Calm down! Do you know what they were doing? Right under my roof! I'm gonna kill both those faggots!"

The hair on the back of my neck stood on end. I had never been so terrified before. He really meant it! He really wanted to kill us both!

"Jeffery! Go downstairs! Cool off! Then we'll discuss this!" I'd never heard my mom speak with such authority. Her tone of voice scared the shit out of me and it wasn't even directed toward me. Mom brooked no argument. Dad glared at me with a look of pure hatred and stomped off downstairs. Mom turned to me.

"Honey." Her questioning, sympathetic voice melted my heart. I burst into tears and hugged her close. My whole world was gone!

"Honey, what happened?" I was crying too hard to answer her. She stepped to the bathroom door. "Taylor, it's all right, you can come out Taylor." He didn't answer, but I could hear him crying inside. Mom came back to me and sat on the bed.

"Mark, honey, what happened?"

Between sobs I told her, about everything. About me being gay, about being in love with Tay, and about what dad had walked in on. I'd never had to tell my mom anything so hard in all my life. Most kids cringe when they think of talking to their parents about sex. That was nothing compared to what I was telling my mom. I couldn't believe I had the courage to speak the words. To her credit, she listened without comment, but I could tell that what she was hearing was tearing her up inside. I was breaking her heart. I was telling her that her son was gay and was having sex with another boy. I couldn't bare to imagine what she thought of me.

"But Mark, you have a girlfriend."

"It's all a fake," I explained, "Me and Laura, Taylor and Steph, we just pretended so no one would suspect us. Everyone thinks me and Tay have girlfriends, so they don't suspect that we're boyfriends."

Mom grew real quiet. She looked at me with disapproval. She tried to hide it, but I could read it in her eyes.

"I don't understand this Mark. You're such a fine young man, so handsome, so athletic, you could have any girl you want."

"Mom, I don't want any girl. That's the point. I'm gay Mom." My mother just couldn't accept the fact that I was gay.

"You're just confused."

"No! I'm not! I'm gay Mom, okay! That's just the way it is!" I couldn't believe what I was saying to my own mother. That thought kept going through my mind over and over.

"I, I don't... I can't..." My mom just couldn't comprehend what I was.

"Mom, try to understand, this is what I am. This is me. I couldn't change it if I wanted to, and I don't want to. I love Tay." There was a long, silent pause. I couldn't hear Taylor crying in the bathroom anymore. I hoped he was all right.

"Mark, I don't really understand all this. I can't say that I approve. I just don't know what to think."

Mom was really stunned, but who could blame her? I wished that she'd hold me close and tell me that everything was okay, that she loved me as I was, but she didn't. She didn't say anything for a long time. After a few moments, she got up and walked to the bathroom door once more.

"Taylor, honey, open the door. No one is going to hurt you."

I heard the lock click and the door opened. Taylor came out with a towel wrapped around his waist. My mom looked at him with disapproval, even disgust. It made me angry to see her look at the one I loved like that. I guess I should have been thankful that she saved my life. Taylor pulled on his boxers while still wearing the towel. He let it drop to the floor and then dressed.

"I think you'd better leave now." said mom. Her voice wasn't angry, but it wasn't very sympathetic either. Taylor's eyes were bloodshot from crying and tear streaks ran down his face. He looked at the door in fear. I didn't blame him. I wouldn't have walked downstairs with my father sitting down there either. Mom read his thoughts.

"I'll walk you out Taylor, and I'll talk to you later Mark."

Taylor's eyes met mine. He looked much as I must have, like someone who's entire world had been laid waste. I could still read the love in his eyes however and I drew strength from that. Mom led him downstairs.

From my bedroom window, I watched Taylor depart. My heart nearly broke as he walked away. I felt like all my hopes and dreams were leaving with him. I imagined that he was glad to escape from my house. I sure wished I could. As Taylor disappeared into the distance, I heard my parents yelling downstairs. They had argued before, but never so violently. I laid on my bed and cried into my pillow. I knew they were arguing about me. My God, why had this happened to me, to us?

I was so afraid, and felt so alone. I didn't know what was going to happen. I no longer feared for my life, but I didn't know what to expect. I was afraid that they'd kick me out, then where would I go? What would I do? I didn't have any money, no where to turn. Sure, Tay would be there for me, but still... Taylor, he was all I had to hold onto. My love for him was all that kept me sane. I drew strength from it. I loved Taylor and he loved me, that's all that really mattered after all.

Still, I'd never been in such a mess before. I couldn't even imagine anything happening that could be worse. I lay there thinking, wanting to fall asleep to escape the nightmare that was my life, but sleep would not come. I was too tormented in mind and spirit to be able to escape that way.

My stomach growled. I was hungry, very hungry. I hadn't had anything since breakfast, but I wasn't about to go downstairs. It was but a small addition to my misery however. It hardly mattered. I couldn't handle all that had happened, I just couldn't. It was far too much. Thoughts of killing myself went through my mind. Maybe it would have been better if my dad had killed me. Death seemed like the only real escape. I was half out of my mind with fear and sorrow. I wasn't thinking straight. I wanted out. I really wanted to die. I went so far as to look in my medicine cabinet to see if I could find anything that would do the job. Maybe, if I took all that was there? I didn't know.

I mentally slapped myself. No, that was not the way. It just wasn't. I worried about Taylor, what if he was thinking along the same lines. I couldn't bear that, but no, he'd quickly come to the same realization that I had. Suicide was not the answer. That was not something to even be considered when there was someone you loved and someone that loved you.

Later that evening mom came up to my room and brought me some supper. She talked to me for a long time, but not much had changed. She just couldn't accept the fact that I was gay. At least she tried to understand. Her disapproval hurt me. When I looked into her eyes I read disappointment there, along with confusion and distaste. The knowledge that my own mother looked on me as a disappointment, as some kind of abnormality, cut into me like a dagger. The way she looked at me made me want to crawl under a rock and die. I guess it could have been worse, she could have reacted more like my father.

"Your father and I have discussed it and you're not to see Taylor anymore."

"What?" I said. My mouth was hanging open. I was almost in a state of disbelief, and yet I guess I should have expected it. I hadn't really thought about it. I wasn't exactly thinking straight after all. If I had been, I would have known it was coming. It was a typical parental reaction. It didn't make it any easier to take however.

"He isn't welcome here and we don't want you hanging around with him."

I thought about saying something like "If he isn't welcome here, then I'm not either", but I decided it best not to dig myself in any deeper. I was already in enough trouble.

"I thought you liked Tay. All you've been saying is how nice a boy he is."

"Your father and I don't like the influence he has over you. We…"

"What? You think I'm gay because of Taylor? I was gay a long time before Taylor came along!"

"I don't want to hear it Mark! He isn't welcome here." It was pretty clear she didn't want to hear anything about me being gay. She just wanted to ignore the whole thing. I guess she thought if she didn't hear about it, it wasn't real.

"But mom! I love Tay! I can't not see him!"

"That's final Mark! You are not to see him."

I knew better than to argue, it wouldn't get me anywhere. I also knew damn well that I would see him. No one would keep me from seeing Tay!

"I called Taylor's mother and talked with her,"

"You did what?" My mouth actually gaped open. I was in a state of shock and disbelief. I couldn't believe she'd done that. My heart broke with the betrayal. At that moment I knew I'd never trust my parents again.

"I discussed it with her and we decided it's best for the two of you not to see each other again."

I couldn't believe what was happening to me. It just didn't seem possible. I really would have killed myself right then and there had I not known full well that Tay and I would be together. No one would keep me from him and I knew Tay wouldn't let anyone keep him away from me. They'd have to kill us both to keep us apart.

Mom left soon after that. There wasn't much more to say. I was hurt, devastated, furious beyond belief. The mix of emotions running through my head were about to make it explode. My heart ached for Taylor. I could just imagine him coming home to find out his parents knew all about what we'd been doing. Taylor was so sensitive. It must have been a nightmare for him. The one thing we'd feared was happening. Our secret was out. I wondered how his parents were treating him. My stomach growled again. I was starving. I wolfed down the supper mom brought me. At least my jailers fed me!

Needless to say I didn't sleep much that night. When I did drift off from exhaustion, the hellish scenes of being discovered by my father played over and over in my head. Only when it was nearly time to get up did I really fall asleep. As I drifted off for the final time, all I could think about was that my worse nightmare had come true.

13 The Vampires are Revealed

The door to my bedroom opened. My father stood glaring down at Taylor and I. We were naked, my father had a shotgun. He raised it, and pulled the trigger...

"Mark, Mark!"

My mom had to shake me to bring me to consciousness. When I did awaken, I shrank back from her violently. My heart was in my throat. It took a few moments for the dreams to clear from my head. My mother left without saying anything further. What was there to say?

I was exhausted, but I sure as hell didn't want to stay in that house any longer than was necessary. Dad was already gone when I came downstairs, although he was usually around for a while before he left for work. He obviously didn't want to see me. That was fine by me. I didn't want to have anything to do with him either. I didn't even really want to be around my mom. I knew what she thought of me, and it hurt. It broke my heart to know that my own mother disapproved of me, thought I was unnatural. Along with the heartbreak was anger. The way my parents had decided to keep me from Taylor make me fucking furious! How could my own parents treat me like that?

I ate quickly and got the hell out of there. I wished more than anything that I had my own place and a job, but I was trapped. School was a sanctuary. It was familiar and filled with my friends, and Tay. I looked for him when I arrived, but couldn't find him anywhere. I hoped he was okay.

Laura found me. She never failed to search me out before class.

"Mark, what's wrong? You look terrible."

I didn't realize my mood showed so easily on my face. My eyes were still bloodshot and I was tired, but I'd looked like that before. Laura was picking up on my crushed spirit. I couldn't tell her the whole truth, so I gave her what part of it I could.

"I had a big fight with my dad last night. He went ballistic."

"What about?"

"I don't really want to talk about it Laura."

She backed off, understanding. She grabbed my hands and comforted me.

"It will be okay Mark, I'm sure it will." She smiled sweetly. I wondered what would happen to that smile if she knew what the fight with my dad was about. It made me feel cold and alone. Her kindness was comforting and yet it only increased the guilt that had been there all along. We had been living a lie. There she was comforting me, while I was taking advantage of her. It made me feel like slime. No, I just couldn't deal with it. I had more than enough on my mind. I forced the guilt from my thoughts. I blocked it from my mind.

I really, really needed to talk to Tay. I spotted him coming toward me and made my apologies to Laura. She seemed to understand. She probably thought it was a guy thing. There wasn't much privacy in the hallway at school, but at least I could check on Taylor.

"You okay?" I asked, deep concern etched in my voice.

"No, not really." he said. He looked at me with tears welling in his eyes. "Your parents called mine. We aren't allowed to see each other anymore."

"I know." I said. "Fuck that! No one is going to keep us apart!" It was hard to keep our voices low enough not to be overheard. Tay smiled at my fury and determination. It was a smile without joy however.

"I won't let them keep me from you Mark." His voice was so earnest and intense that I knew the same fire burned in his heart, that burned within my own.

I wanted to hug him right there in the hall, but it was impossible. I hated the world for making us hide our love for each other. I hated it for keeping me from comforting the one I loved. Why did it have to be that way?

"Tay, we'll get through this. We have each other and that's all that matters."

Taylor shook his head. "Yes" he said meekly. I could tell that he didn't really believe everything would be okay. He looked as if he'd lost hope.

The bell rang. We had to go. We couldn't really talk in the hall anyway.

"Meet me at lunch." I said. "We'll go outside and talk this out. We'll make it Tay."

Taylor weakly smiled. I was really worried about him. I'd never seen him so down. I was pretty depressed and upset too, but Tay looked like he was walking through hell itself. Seeing him in pain hurt me far more than my own suffering ever could. He was the sensitive one. What had happened was hitting him even harder than it was me.

It was hard to concentrate in class. My mind was filled with what had happened and I was so worried about Tay. I kept looking at him during English. He looked like a weak duplicate of himself, a clone without joy or life. As we parted at the end of the period, he drifted off like he wasn't even aware of himself, or his surroundings.

It seemed like lunch-time would never arrive. When it came at last, I rushed to the cafeteria. Taylor was waiting on me. We walked outside where no one could hear us.

"What did your parents do?" I asked.

"They freaked," he said. The look in Taylor's eyes was downright frightening. He had the look of someone who had witnessed an atrocity. "My dad called me a fag and told me how bitterly disappointed he was in me. They both acted like my being gay was some kind of crime. Like I was doing it to hurt them. They didn't understand. My dad actually hit me!"

I hadn't noticed it before, but there was a bruise on Taylor's cheek. I wanted to kill his dad for that.

"Oh Taylor." I said. I wanted to caress his cheek, take him in my arms and hug him, but I couldn't. No one could overhear us, but they might see us. Once again, I was angry at the world for keeping me from expressing my love.

"When he hit me, mom yelled at him. She said she wouldn't put up with him hitting me, even if I was a fag."

Taylor looked at me with sorrow in his eyes. He was crying.

"She actually said it just like that… 'even if he is a fag'. My own mother called me a fag!" Tay started crying harder. He was all torn up.

I didn't care if anyone could see us. I took Tay in my arms and hugged him, just for a moment. I loved him and I didn't care what anyone did to me for hugging him. Luckily, no one saw me comforting my boyfriend.

I filled Taylor in on the events at my house. His concern for me quieted his tears. I could tell he cared more about my problems than he did about his own. Just like I cared about his more than mine. We really, really loved each other. Both of us drew strength from that.

We talked the entire lunch period. Comforting each other, trying to deal with the situation. We were there for each other. When the time came to part, we were both still upset, but we knew we'd pull each other through the whole horrible mess, somehow.

I didn't think things could possibly get worse than they already were, but they did get worse, much worse. The events of the night before seemed almost unimportant compared to what happened next. My God, it still terrifies me to even think of it.

That very same afternoon, coach walked into the locker room while we were all dressing for soccer practice. I was just tying my shoes and Taylor was already dressed.

"Boy's we have to discuss something serious."

The whole room got quiet. Coach rarely talked like that and he had never used that tone of voice before. Hell, he never came into the locker room to talk to us at all. Something big was up. Something real big.

"It seems we have a couple of fairies in our midst." he said. "A couple of queers who can't keep their hands off each other."

My face blanched and my heart nearly stopped. Time slowed I could not believe what was happening. It just couldn't be! It couldn't! I looked at Taylor with sheer panic in my eyes and was met by much the same look. All the guys on the team were looking around, or staring at the coach. No one could believe what was going on.

"We have a job to do men. It's up to us to keep these little faggots away from each other. Since they can't control themselves, we have to keep them apart."

I think it was the worst moment of my life, even worse than what happened with my dad the day before. It was like one of those bad dreams where you're at school in nothing but your underwear, but this was far, far worse. My God, I was about to be exposed in front of all my friends. I would have done literally anything to get out of there. I was going out of my mind with fear and panic.

"Everyone take a good look at Mark and Taylor. They're the little homos that you all have to keep an eye on."

All eyes turned to us. There were staring at us like we were some kind of freak show. We'd been outed. At last, they knew we were vampires and they'd destroy us both. I couldn't stand them all staring at me like that. I couldn't take the shocked expressions, the looks of disbelief. I sure as hell wasn't going to just sit there while coach denounced me. My eyes darted around like those of a frightened animal. I felt like a cornered beast. My thoughts were irrational. My mind clutched in terror. I nearly bolted. I nearly forgot all about Taylor in my panic. My eyes met his however and I could read the terror in them. Taylor looked like a doe caught in the headlights of an oncoming car.

I stood, stepped toward him. No one tried to stop me.

"Taylor, let's go."

He arose and followed me. Coach blocked our path. I knocked him to the side. He grabbed my shoulder.

"Don't touch me!" I yelled at him. My tone was so fierce he shrank back from me. He quickly recovered, but by then we were half way out the door. We left all the stares behind. We left all the spectators who were watching the freak show. I was totally panic stricken. I couldn't think about anything except getting the hell out of there.

Taylor stopped dead in his tracks in the gym. I pulled him toward the exit, but he resisted me. I looked at him. His eyes were filled with tears.

"I've just got to be alone." he stammered. "I've just got to think about this. I'm, I'm sorry..." He turned and ran from the gym.

Some of the guys had come out of the locker room. They were staring at me and whispering to each other. They were laughing and I knew it was all about me and Taylor. Devon was looking at me with pure disgust. Seeing that look on the face of one of my closest friends cut into my heart like a sharp knife. He looked around at our team-mates, then back at me. Along with the disgust, there was a self-satisfied smirk on his face.

"I told you guys they were fucking fags. I told you."

I couldn't handle it. I bolted. I ran faster than I'd ever run before, right out of the gym, right out of the school, right to my car. I jumped in and peeled out of the parking lot and didn't slow down until I was far, far away.

I drove around for I don't know how long, my mind racing. It was all over. By the next morning everyone would know. Everyone! I pulled out my hair. How did things come to this? Why hadn't I locked my door? Why did my dad have to walk in on us like that? My God, everyone was going to know. Our secret was out. There was no stopping it. The villages would be out in force soon, stakes in hand, to kill the vampires in their midst. We were revealed. It was all over.

I only just barely managed to keep from intentionally running my car into a light pole. I wanted to die. I wanted to avoid what was to come. I wanted out.I really think I would have done it, if it wasn't for Taylor. Even as I thought of careening my car into a light pole, I saw him in my mind. No, I couldn't do that to him.

What about Taylor? Where was he? What was going through his mind? I was sick with worry over him.

When I finally arrived home, it was late. I was more upset than I'd ever been before. My mom stopped me on the stairs as I went to my room.

"Mark, your father thought he was doing the right thing when he called your coach. I know…"

"What? HE called my coach!" I should have figured it out long before, but I wasn't exactly thinking clearly.

My mom started to explain. I didn't want to hear, no explanation could possibly make up for what he had done.

"I'll never speak to him again!" I shouted, ran up the stairs and slammed my door. I knew my dad was home and that he'd heard everything. I didn't give a damn. I didn't care if he came to my room and beat me. I was through with him. As far as I was concerned, my father was dead.

Mom called me down to supper later. I considered just staying in my room, but I couldn't hold out there forever. I was not a free man. I came downstairs. We were one of those families that always ate in front of the television, unless we had guests. That made it easier to ignore HIM. I barely even spoke to my mother. She wasn't exactly innocent in all that had happened. She had betrayed me almost as much as he had. I felt like I was a Jewish boy being held in Gestapo headquarters. I knew my every movement was being watched. It wouldn't have surprised me if they tapped my phone. Okay, maybe I was being a little paranoid, but I knew what was going through their minds.

After supper I started to leave the house, but my mom stopped me.

"We think it's best if you don't go out for a while." said my mother. The way she said it was so nice, so condescending, it was as if she were telling a six year old child not to go out in the cold without a coat. It made me furious.

"So I'm grounded now too?"

She didn't answer, but I knew it was the case. I turned and walked back upstairs. I closed and locked my door. I picked up the phone and called Tay. Luckily, we both had our own private lines. He didn't answer. That was odd. I assumed he was under the same house arrest that I was. Our parents seemed pretty together on everything. They probably had little meetings on how to keep us apart.

My heart nearly stopped when there was a knock at my window. I turned around in a flash. It was Tay!

I quickly opened up and pulled him in.

"Are you out of your fucking mind?" I hissed between clinched teeth. I had no idea what would happen if my parents caught Tay in my room. I ran over and checked my door, even though I knew it was locked.

"I just came to get you. Let's go somewhere and talk."

I shut out my lights and followed Taylor out the window. We climbed down the trellis and dropped to the ground. Without a word, Tay led me away from the house. I followed him for a couple of blocks, right to the old Graymoor place, Verona, Indiana's most notorious haunted house. It had been abandoned for years, every since old man Graymoor went nuts and hacked up his entire family with an ax. Old man Graymoor was Verona's Lizzie Borden. I couldn't believe it when Taylor opened the gate and walked toward it.

"Are you crazy?" I asked.

He just grabbed me by the shirt and pulled me forward. I reluctantly followed him. I didn't like being there. I didn't really believe it was haunted, but it was a murder house and it gave me the creeps. No one ever went in there, not even full grown men in the daylight. I bet no one had been there since the mob that hanged old man Graymoor, and that was nearly a hundred years before.

Taylor led me inside. The heavy carved door creaked in protest. The light was dim in there, the place was dilapidated and looked like it was ready to cave in. A hundred years of disuse had taken it's toll. Talk about lack of upkeep. There was a painting of the Graymoor family hanging over the mantle, water stained from the leaking roof. The whole place made the hair on the back of my neck stand on end.

Taylor turned on a flashlight. I looked at him. In the dim light I could see tears flooding his eyes and running down his cheeks. I forgot all about the painting, the murders, and the ghosts.

I pulled him to me, and hugged him tight, as I had wanted to so often that day. Tay sobbed with his head on my shoulder. I ran my hand through his hair, trying to comfort him. I held him as if I was protecting him from all the world.

"I'm sorry I ran like that. I just couldn't take it." he explained. "I was more than half out of my mind. I just had to get away and think. I'm so sorry I left you."

I took his face in my hands and stared into his eyes.

"Tay, it's okay. I understand. We both needed to be alone for a little while to think things out."

"They just sat there looking at us!" said Tay. "They didn't say a word. Not a one of them spoke up for us. I've never been so humiliated in all my life! They just looked at us like we were some kind of monsters! I know what they were thinking. I could read it in their eyes! Why couldn't they just leave us alone? What have we done that's so bad? What did we do to deserve this?"

I held Tay as he sobbed uncontrollably once more. My heart ached for him, and myself. My God! How had all this happened? It was almost unreal, like something on some movie. It couldn't really be happening to us!

I was crying too. Tay and I held onto each other and bawled our eyes out. I didn't feel one bit bad about crying. We weren't pansies for crying. Anybody in our situation would have done the same. When we had both quieted a bit, I took Tay by the chin and pulled his face to mine. I kissed him and hugged him tight. Taylor kissed me back. We just stood there, kissing and hugging each other, trying to blot out the rest of the world.

We stayed together as long as we dared. We didn't fear the ghosts, but we knew there'd be hell to pay if our parents found out we were gone. I walked Tay home in the comforting cloak of darkness, holding his hand, lending him support. I kissed him goodnight, then walked home. I slipped into my house, or should I say prison, climbing the trellis and entering through the window. I climbed into bed and actually cried myself to sleep. I was overwhelmed by all that had happened and I felt that I had but one friend in all the world. Unless you've experienced it for yourself, and God help you if you do, there is no way you can comprehend how ultimately dreadful it is to be singled out, ridiculed, and hated. It was all the worse for being undeserved. I mean, if I had killed someone or something, I would have figured I had it coming, but all I did was dare to love another boy. Why does loving someone have to be a crime?

14 Into the Lion's Den

I awoke the next morning to a few moments of blissful ignorance. In the time it took my head to clear, I was actually unaware of the hellish nightmare that my life had become. As soon as the remnants of sleep had been cleared away, the full weight of what had transpired, and what was to come, fell on me with it's crushing weight. I had never wanted to stay in bed so desperately in all my life. I didn't see how I could possibly face my friends (if I still had any), my class-mates, or my team-mates.

I seriously considered just running away. Taylor and I could go somewhere no one knew us, get jobs, and… No, I knew that wasn't the answer even as the thought entered my head. In that direction lay a bleak future: minimum wage jobs, poverty, living in a world of strangers, and only God knew what else. I was sharp enough to know that the world is a cruel place with no sympathy for those down on their luck. Two eighteen year old boys could not make it on their own. Death would be a preferable option to the life Tay and I would have if we exiled ourselves from Verona. As bleak as it was, here was where our future lay, at least for the time being, at least until we were older.

I forced myself to sit up on the edge of my bed. I just sat there in my box-ers, lacking the will to get up and get ready. I stretched my arms over my head. I felt ridiculous. I had to go on. I stood and forced myself to shower and dress for school. "God help me through this day" I silently prayed as I pulled on my clothes. I was going to need all the help I could get to make it through what was to come.

I wondered what Mrs. Campbell, the woman who threw such a fit about Mr. Hahn's "pro gay" poster (as she called it), would have to say about me and Taylor. No doubt she'd blame it on that poster and argue that if only it had been taken down sooner we wouldn't have turned gay. What a bitch. I wondered what Katie would think after she learned that I was gay. I guess being outed solved the whole problem of Laura's mom having the hots for me. Laura! Fuck! With all that had been going on, I had almost forgotten about her and Steph. Was there no end to this nightmare?

I entered the kitchen. Both my parents were there. My dad didn't speak to me, didn't even look at me. I had been dis-owned. It cut me to the quick, and yet, it was just as well. He had betrayed me, exposed me to my entire soccer team, and ultimately to the entire school. I had nothing to say to him, nothing, not then, not ever.

My mother was far from innocent, but she had protected me and was probably the reason I hadn't been kicked out of the house. As much as her lack of acceptance hurt, she had stood up for me in her own way. In time, perhaps, things would be okay between us. I was civil to mom, if not too warm. The tension in our house was so thick it was practically a tangible, visible thing. I grabbed a donut and walked out the door. I was beginning what would probably be the worst day of my life, assuming anything could possibly be worse than the day before. The villagers knew Taylor and I were vampires and the stalking would begin. I half expected us to be chased through town by our class-mates, waving torches and wooden stakes as they pursued us.

It started before I even walked into school; the stares, the looks, the whispering as I passed. Tay and I were undoubtedly the talk of the school. We were the freak show, the school fags. I could clearly sense the disapproval that I expected. I could read it in the eyes of many of those I passed, not that anyone met my gaze. Few of my classmates seemed to be able to look me in the eyes.

What I felt most of all was a sense of awkwardness and ill ease. That feeling was all around me and far more pronounced than the sense of disapproval. Most disapproved, but everyone seemed to feel uncomfortable around me, everyone. When I passed it was like something unnatural had just went by. Conversations halted, boys tensed, girls looked at me with confusion and curiosity. It was almost as if I was from another world. It was all subtle, but it was as real as if it had all been shouted at me.

The worst were those few who not only looked at me, but glared. Without exception the glaring ones were male. I could read the hatred and contempt in their eyes. The moment I was outed, I became their enemy, even though I'd never done anything to harm them. I was the same boy I was before they knew I was gay, and yet everything was changed. Those who once admired me, now looked on me with contempt. I'm sure not a few delighted in my fall. They couldn't wait to drive a stake through the vampire's heart.

I tried not to let it get to me, but it did. The stares, the silence, the disapproval, the sense of ill ease, all of it cut me to the quick. I fought hard not to let my feelings show. Truth to be known I was on the verge of breaking into tears. Now wouldn't that have been great? I could just image what the glaring boys would have had to say about the crying fag.

I didn't give them the satisfaction. I steeled myself against it all and walked into school. If anything, it was worse inside. The mix of emotions gained power as they were confined within a smaller space. My classmates actually stepped back from me as I passed. Old friends pretended they didn't see me or acknowledged my presence less than they would that of a stranger. No one walked up to me. No one said "hi".The day before, I'd been a reasonably popular soccer jock, now I was the school fag. I caught a few satisfied smirks from those who reveled in what had happened to me. They were ecstatic that my life was ruined. The world was a very cruel place.

I scanned the faces, but I didn't see Tay anywhere. I wondered if he'd come to school after what had happened. I wondered where he was, and if he was okay. As difficult as my situation was, I worried about him even more. I loved him so very much and it hurt me to think what he must be going through. I yearned to hold him in my arms and comfort him once more.

I neared my locker. She was standing there. I had been expecting a confrontation with Laura, and was not looking forward to it in the least. Laura was waiting for me with crossed arms, her expression hurt and angry. She was nearly in tears. She was one of the few that looked me in the eye, and I did not care for what I saw there at all. I faced her, walked toward her. I had hurt her and I knew it. I did not deserve to be hated for what I was, but I did deserve her wrath. I had deceived her, used her. No matter how good of a time I tried to show her, no matter how well I treated her, or what I bought her, it didn't alter what I'd done to her. I had never meant for her to know. I had never meant for others to know. But I had known the risk was there, and I had taken it without consulting her, without warning her of the danger. I had committed her to my course as surely as I had committed myself, and now she suffered for my mistake. Whatever she did to me, I deserved it.

I stood, facing her. I wanted to tell her how sorry I was, but the words would not come. No one stood near us, but a crowd was milling around, ready to watch the show. Her friends, our classmates, and so many more, it made it that much more difficult on us both.

"I'm sorry." It was all I could force out, nothing else would come.

Laura slapped me hard across the face. The pain was intense, but I barely flinched. I deserved it.

"You bastard!" she hissed, her anger mixed with tears. "You bastard! How could you humiliate me like this? Did I mean anything to you at all? Or were you just playing me for a fool? Was it fun Mark? Did you enjoy ruining my life? Did you find it funny, knowing I was dating a fag?"

Her words cut into me like a scalpel slicing up my flesh, cutting it's way to my heart.

"I never meant to hurt you Laura."

"Never meant to hurt me!" she was practically screeching. "Never meant to hurt me! God help whoever you do intend to hurt! You made a fool out of me! You took advantage of me! What kind of monster are you? You pretended to date me when you had a boyfriend! What did you do, sleep with him after you took me home? I never want to see you again!"

She kneed me right in the nuts, as hard as she possibly could. I doubled over and fell to the floor. I was in agony. I squirmed on the floor moaning, putting on a show for all those around me. I'd never felt pain like that before.

I could feel everyone looking at me. I could feel Laura staring at me.

"I hope for your boyfriend's sake I didn't damage anything!" Laura snorted and laughed derisively, then stomped away in a huff. I pulled myself to my feet. No one offered to help me. I could barely stand. I gathered my books and limped toward class. Would my balls ever stop hurting? The physical pain cut through my emotional turmoil for a few minutes. My balls hurt too much for my mind to consider anything else. As I neared my first period class, a couple of football players slammed into me, knocking my books everywhere.

"Sorry Princess," they mockingly called to me, "hope you didn't chip a nail." They continued down the hall with self-satisfied smirks and wicked laughter. I wanted to just lay into them, but I could barely walk. Even if I hadn't been so debilitated, taking on the two of them would have been suicide. In my present state, that didn't seem like such a bad idea. I fought to maintain control. I didn't know whether I wanted to shout in anger or cry. I did neither, but walked into class, sat down heavily, and attempted to ignore the icy atmosphere.

Even in the classroom, I felt my classmates looking at me. There was no escape from all those eyes. Even my teacher was gazing at me with the now familiar curious/shocked look. Like most, he tried to conceal his efforts to watch me, but he couldn't help but look at me. I felt like I was a traffic accident or something.

Everyone looked at me like I was some kind of freak. I could not evade detection. I could not escape from prying eyes. I felt like I was living my life under a microscope. Was this what it was going to be like? Was this what my life had become? An overpowering desire to crawl under a rock and hide seeped into my very bones. I felt like screaming at everyone to quit staring at me, but more attention was not what I needed. It was a nightmare!

I was about to snap. I just couldn't take it. The effort of maintaining control was becoming too much. I finally did snap. I'd held out for over an hour, but then I couldn't bear it anymore. I was walking down the hallway between first and second period, trying to block out everything around me, when Randy had to open his big mouth.

"How's it going fag boy?"

I couldn't take it. I lost control. I turned and smashed him in the mouth. He fell to the floor. I reached down and grabbed him. I was going to pull him to his feet and beat the shit out of him. Someone grabbed me from behind. I shook them off.

"Hold it right there Mr. Bailey!" I froze. It was Mr. Montgomery, our assistant principal. I turned and faced him.

"Did you hear what he called me?"

By the look on his face, I could tell he didn't care.

"Did you?" He ignored my question.

"Come on." He grabbed me by the collar and dragged me to his office. I noticed a lot of my class-mates smirking. They thought it was funny as hell.

Mr. Montgomery dropped me into a chair and looked at me with stern disapproval.

"Did you hear what he called me?" I repeated. "He called me 'fag boy'."

"Listen," he said in his stern voice. "You've chosen your life style and you're just going to have to deal with it. If you do the things you've obviously been

doing, you're going to have to expect to be ridiculed for it. " I couldn't believe
he said that.

"But..."

"I don't want to hear it Mr. Bailey. I'm giving you three weeks detention."

"Three weeks! That's not fair. He called me 'fag boy'. What about him? I..."

"Enough!"

Mr. Montgomery practically shoved me out of his office. He treated me like
a piece of garbage he was dumping on the curb. I was mad as hell. I got punished for defending myself and Mr. Montgomery didn't do a damn thing to
Randy. He acted like I deserved being treated like a piece of shit, like it was all
my doing. Detention sucked. At my school detention meant being stuck in
school for three hours on Saturday. Fuck that! I just wouldn't go!

At lunch, no one sat by me, no one. They treated me like a leper, all of them!
I felt betrayed. Didn't even one of my friends have the balls to at least sit with
me? Had they all forsaken me?

I didn't see Taylor all day. That was unusual as we generally sought each other
out, especially at lunch. I kept looking for him, but didn't see him once. I hoped
he was okay, not for the last time.

15 Living in a Glass House

I stood outside the locker room, summoning my courage to walk in. I had bolted the day before, but I'd be damned if I'd let coach and a few others keep me from playing soccer. I think walking into that locker room was one of the hardest things I ever had to do. I didn't know what would await me inside. I'd been nervous about it all day. Well, that's not quite true. I'd been through so much during the day that the nervousness about what would happen at soccer practice was often driven from my mind.

I stepped through the door. I felt like a convicted criminal stepping up to the gallows. All eyes turned to me as I entered. I could feel coach stare at me, boring holes into the back of my head. He didn't say anything to me however. A few of my team-mates backed off as I passed and all of them were looking at me. A couple of them were naked and hurried to pull on their uniforms. Guys were quickly dressing all around me, or were afraid to undress. That made my heart ache. I bit my lip and opened my locker. I kept my mind on changing my clothes, trying to block out those around me. My team-mates turned back to what they were doing, but they were still watching me. A few were glaring at me, but most of them were trying to act as if nothing was out of the ordinary. They weren't very successful.

I could feel how ill at ease most of my team-mates were with me in the room. I guess I couldn't really blame them. To be honest, checking out all the naked and half naked guys in the locker room was a secret pleasure of mine. Well, I guess not so secret anymore, but before I was exposed it was an arousing thrill.

I could enjoy the scenery and none the wiser. My straight team-mates would have given their eye teeth to enjoy that privilege in the girl's locker room.

I didn't dare check out any of the guys now. I couldn't so much as look at them. Not so much because I was afraid of getting belted in the mouth, but because I didn't want to make them any more uncomfortable than they already were. It hurt me to think that my team-mates didn't trust me. Maybe I deserved that a little, I had checked out their young bodies now and then, but I hadn't really done anything wrong. All I had done was look.

I was tying my shoes when Brandon and Jon walked up to me. I felt myself tense as they neared. I was afraid. They stood there for a moment and I looked up. I wasn't sure what to expect. My whole world was filled with uncertainty. I felt like there was nothing, and no one, I could depend on, except Taylor of course.

"I'm glad you came back Mark." said Brandon. "I'm sorry some guys have to be so judgmental." He glanced around the locker room pointedly.

"Yeah," said Jon. "We wouldn't have stood a chance against the Trojans this weekend without you."

"Thanks." I said, with more genuine feeling than I'd ever felt before. They were the only two who had given me any kind of support the entire day. Those guys didn't know what it meant to me to have someone just talk to me like I wasn't a freak. The mood in the locker room seemed to ease just a bit. Some small fraction of the tension was gone. Things were far from normal, but my two friends had built a bridge that would help us all cross unfamiliar territory. I was relieved to know that I still had a couple of friends. I was beginning to think all of them had forsaken me. Any friend that stood by my side now was a friend indeed.

As difficult as it all was for me, I knew that it had to be hard on my team-mates as well. How did one react when one discovered that someone one thought one knew was something totally unexpected? Well, maybe not totally unexpected, but close enough.

A few of the guys still looked at me with open disapproval and disgust, but it seemed that most would at least let me be and a rare few would even accept me as I was. Things were going to be hard, very hard, but not so impossible as I at first suspected.

As these thoughts were running through my mind, Taylor entered. The guys looked him over too, but not nearly as much as they stared at me when I entered. I guess I had kind of broken the ice. A couple of guys even said "hi" to him. I didn't like the looks others were giving him however. It made me want to just lay into them. I couldn't stand the condemnation, not of someone I loved so very much. Our position would not be helped by me getting into another fight however, so I swallowed my anger and focused instead on making things easier for Tay.

"Hey Taylor." I said. "Ready for practice?"

"Only if we don't do those damned calve-killer exercises again."

I could tell his spirits were low, but he was trying to keep going, just as I was.

I expected someone to make a smart remark, say something about me talking to my boyfriend, but no one did. Maybe the way Brandon and Jon were standing there protectively had something to do with it. I'd never forget how those guys stood by me if I lived to be a hundred.

Practice was tough, both physically and mentally. I didn't mind the physical part, it helped me to concentrate on soccer instead of my situation. The mental part was far more difficult. Despite the open acceptance of a few, and the neutrality of others, there were still many of my team-mates that just didn't want either Tay, or myself, to be there. I could read it in their eyes and their expressions.

The worst of them weren't subtle at all. I was knocked on my ass repeatedly. Getting hit was not unusual during practice, but when it happened over and over it was obvious that it was no accident. I heard a lot of things murmured under the breath as well: "fairy", "faggot", "queer", "sissy", and all the rest. I tried not to let it get to me, but it did. Team-mates were supposed to stick together, but as far as some of the guys were concerned, I wasn't worthy of being on the team anymore.

A few of them wouldn't even pass me the ball during practice. I'd be wide open while everyone else was covered. Other guys would be yelling for the guy with the ball to pass it to me, but he just acted like he didn't hear, didn't see. It was like I wasn't even there. I even heard one of my team-mates mutter, "I'm not passing to the fairy." to one of his buddies. They both laughed at me like I wasn't even there. God that hurt. It was all getting to be too much.

After practice was even worse. When I walked into the showers, most of the guys in there beat a hasty retreat. Only Taylor and a very few others stayed. I smiled wanly at Tay. He knew what I was going through, no one better. We both showered quickly and got out of there. Most of the guys would not go into the showers until we had left. The most militant of my team-mates wouldn't even undress until both Taylor and I were completely out of the locker room. It made me feel distinctly unwanted and unwelcome. The guys that were pulling that crap didn't care, they wanted me and Taylor to feel like outcasts. That's how they thought of us and they wanted both of us off the team. If treating us like shit would do the job, then that was fine by them. I was thankful that most of our team-mates weren't so cruel or homophobic. I genuinely appreciated the handful that stood by us.

Taylor was going through everything I was. It was comforting in a way, and yet it also made it worse. I detested thinking about the one I loved experiencing such pain. As bad as it was for me, thinking about Tay suffering was the hardest part. I just couldn't stand watching someone I cared for so much suffer like that. I finally understood what my father said to me when I was six years old and very, very sick. He told me he wished he could be sick instead of me. At the time I didn't understand why anyone would want to feel like I did, but now I understood. My suffering was harder for my father to bear than his own would have been. I was willing to bet he'd no longer feel the same way. I knew he wouldn't. He was personally responsible for most of my suffering. He was the one that had exposed me to all my friends. He was the one who destroyed my life.

Tay met me outside the locker room. As soon as he stepped out we could hear some of our team-mates yelling at each other. Our few "supporters" were chewing out the "homophobes" and getting ragged on for it. I really appreciated those few guys standing up for me and Tay. I know it wasn't easy. It showed me who our real friends were.

I looked at Taylor. I could tell he had been through one hell of a day.

"Come on,' I said. "I'll walk you home."

"Didn't you drive?"

"No car, my parents took my keys. They think it'll keep me from seeing you."

"Oh."

I turned to Taylor and looked him straight in the eyes.

"Nothing will keep me from seeing you Tay, nothing."

"And no one will keep me away from you." he said.

That little exchange made me feel better. I knew already that we were both determined to stick together, but hearing it spoken out loud gave that determination strength.

Taylor and I were getting plenty of looks as we walked together. Mostly it was just curious gazes. Everyone seemed so shocked to find out that Taylor and I were gay. I guess we didn't fit the stereotypes that they'd built up in their heads. Gay guys were supposed to be effeminate, soft spoken, and meek. Tay and I certainly didn't fit that description! We were jocks, loud, and wild, at least on the soccer field. I guess we kind of upset everyone's notions of what gay guys were like. Tough shit, they'd just have to learn that there were all types of gay guys, just like there were all types of guys.

Some of the looks were filled with hatred and contempt. I'd always hidden what I was because I knew there were such feelings out there, but actually experiencing the prejudice and animosity was an overwhelming experience. It's one thing to hear about such incidents, it's quite another to be on the receiving end. It was hard to believe that some people actually hated me and Tay just because we were gay.

"Faggots!" A car whizzed by, filled with high school guys I didn't recognize.

Taylor and I tried to ignore them and tried to ignore the people on the street who looked at us questioningly. Never before had I realized the value of being able to walk down the street unknown and unmolested. I guessed those days were over for good.

Two blocks from Taylor's house we said goodbye and went our separate ways. It would have been great if we could have studied together the way we once did, but I wasn't welcome in his home anymore, nor he in mine. I walked home alone, wishing the nightmare was all a dream and that I would wake up to find all my troubles gone. It's funny, my life before being outed was far from perfect. I was so lonely before I met Taylor and there were so many problems to handle when we started dating, but looking back those times seemed a golden age.

16 An Unexpected Friend

My second day as a vampire writhing in the sunlight was only slightly less traumatic than the first. As unpleasant as it was, at least I knew what to expect. There was no dramatic scene with Laura either, although she glared at me with pure hatred whenever our paths crossed. My balls still ached a little from when she'd kneed me. It was a deserved reminder of what I'd done. Of the whole mess, what I'd done to Laura is what I felt truly bad about. I didn't deserve the taunts, the glares, or the discrimination, but I did deserve every bit of anger she directed at me. I was truly sorry for what I'd done to her.

A few more of my classmates spoke to me on the second day, but the number was depressingly low. Most were just too uncomfortable around me to act normal and some obviously despised me. I could understand the way Laura felt, but I didn't deserve the hatred of others. It was mainly the guys who were down on me. Boys that I had considered good friends just a short time before treated me like I was some kind of traitor. It was like they had expected me to go around wearing a sign that said I was gay or something. They reminded me of a bunch of fucking Nazi's, hating anyone who was different and pinning all that was wrong with the world on them.

I always knew I had to keep my sexual preference a secret, but I never expected to be treated like a convict by guys I'd considered my friends. Things changed so quickly. One day they were slapping me on the back and telling me how awesome a soccer player I was, the next day they treated me like I'd killed their dog. It was hard to believe that my "friends" could turn on me that fast, and for so little reason. It made me appreciate the few friends that did stick with me all the more.

The girls were more accepting. I didn't sense any hatred from them, except Laura of course and a few of her friends. Hell, I'd have been pissed too if I was them. I wouldn't have appreciated someone taking advantage of one of my friends like that.

Mostly the girls were curious or just looked at me like some kind of attraction at a circus. I had the feeling that most of them were just really surprised and didn't know how to handle it. Some of them had flirted with me before and I'm sure a few of them were attracted to me. Finding out I was into guys and not girls must have been unsettling for them, but hey we all had problems.

The girls didn't particularly make me feel at ease, but at least they weren't sneering at me and calling me fag or fairy as I walked past. I got tired of the name calling real quick, but there wasn't much I could do about it. My instinct was to whip everyone's ass that dared to call me queer or homo, but there were just too many of them. I couldn't fight dozens of guys and I'd just get into more trouble if I got into another fight. So I just took it. Most of the time the names were said under the breath, or disguised in a cough. It was amazing how many guys had to cough when I was around. It didn't really matter how it was done. Being persecuted was not a pleasant experience.

I sat down alone at lunch. I dreaded it. Trying to eat while the entire world is watching you is not a lot of fun. Taylor sat down across from me. That drew plenty of comments from the Nazi's, that's what I'd come to call those who ragged on me and Taylor because we were gay. I could hear their snide comments in the distance, all concerning what Taylor and I did when we were alone. The harassment was hard to take, but Taylor and I weren't about to avoid each other because of what someone might say. We'd already been marked as fags and spending time together wasn't going to make it any worse. Still, it wasn't easy.

I felt a little better when Brandon and Jon sat down by us. Those guys had really taken up for us the day before at soccer practice. They were real friends. They acted as if nothing had changed. I can't describe how good that made me feel. It wasn't long before Ethan, Jordan, and Matt joined us too. That surprised me a little bit. Up to that point none of them had said anything derogatory to me or Tay, but they'd been keeping their distance. I guess it just took them a little time. I didn't blame them for that. I never appreciated my friends more than I did at that moment. Taylor looked at me and smiled. I knew he was thinking the same thing.

When Steve sat down near me, I was really surprised. I looked at him and he returned my gaze. He gave me a look that told me he didn't care if I was gay or not. I'd won his respect when we'd fought, and my sexual preference didn't change that.

Just when I was starting to get a little bit comfortable, things got unpleasant again. I was eating a cheese burger and talking to Tay and some of the other guys when I heard the familiar voice of one of my former friends behind me.

"Looking for some recruits faggots?"

I knew who it was before I even turned around, it was Devon. Most of the Nazi's talked shit under their breath, or yelled it from a distance, but this was Hitler himself. Devon was bound and determined to rip into me and Taylor as much as he possibly could. He delighted in our pain and sought to be the cause of it as much as possible. I turned around. His words were a direct attack. I wasn't going to take any crap from him.

My eyes had barely met his when I heard Jon and Brandon stand up behind me. Devon's eyes quickly turned to them and he held up his hands.

"I'm not saying anything about you guys. I know you wouldn't go queer."

"Shut the fuck up Devon!" yelled Brandon.

"Why are you standing up for this faggot?" asked Devon. "For God's sake he's a fucking queer!"

"That's enough Devon!" said Brandon. "You're not calling any friend of mine those names. Apologize or I'm going to kick your ass right now." Brandon meant it and was quite capable of it. Jon was standing by his side and looked more than willing to help, although Brandon would not have needed it. Ethan, Jordan, and Matt didn't say a word, but the way they glared at Devon made their position clear.

Devon looked at Steve and Steve blew him off like he wasn't even there. I had to fight to keep a little smile from turning up the edges of my mouth.

Devon snorted. I could tell he wanted to say something particularly nasty, but he thought better of it. He knew he was seconds away from getting his ass whipped.

"Sorrr-ee!" he said, clearly without meaning it. He beat a hasty retreat.

The scene had attracted a little crowd and all heads were turned our way.

"What are you looking at!" said Jon. "Get a life."

Everyone turned quickly back to their own business.

"Thanks guys." I said.

"Yeah, thanks." echoed Taylor.

"No problem." said Brandon. "You guys shouldn't have to put up with that shit. What business of theirs is your personal life anyway? I'm not saying I understand it, but you're my friends and that's all that matters."

"Yeah!" said Jon jumping up once again and flexing his muscles as if he was ready to fight off an army. I couldn't help but laugh and neither could anyone else. It was the first time I could remember laughing in a long time. Too bad all of my friends couldn't have been like those guys.

I walked Taylor home again that afternoon. It was one of the few times we could be more or less alone together. We had to pay for it by being on the receiving end of stares and taunts, but it was worth it. We both drew strength from each other and that's something we desperately needed. Besides, I loved walking with Taylor.

I took my leave of him not far from his house and went my own way. I arrived home and there, waiting on me, was one of the last people I expected to see. It was Jennifer.

"Hi." I said, a bit hesitantly as I approached. I didn't know what to expect from her at all.

"Mark, can we talk?" Her tone was more or less pleasant, which surprised me to no end.

"Sure." I said, curious and just a little suspicious.

"Let's walk." she suggested. We strolled down the street, silent for a while, then she spoke.

"I was really mad at you when you started dating Laura. You weren't really going with her until that night at the bon fire were you?"

"No." I admitted. "I just told you I was seeing someone to get you off me." I continued, I felt like I had to explain. "You were kind of aggressive and I guess you know now that I'm not interested in that kind of thing, you know?"

"You mean with girls?"

"Yes." I said quietly. "Look, Jennifer, you're very attractive, hell you're gorgeous, and if I was into girls, I'd have been thrilled with what was going on that night, but it's just not me. You understand?"

"Yeah, I think I do." She was smiling at me. "I was really upset that night. I didn't understand why a good looking guy like you wasn't interested in me. I was pretty sure you were lying about dating someone. I mean, I'd never seen you with a girl and I'd been watching. Then, when I saw you with Laura, it just didn't make sense. I mean, she's pretty, and nice, but a little too nice you know. She's probably one of those girls that won't do anything before they're married."

"Pretty much." I said.

"But it all makes sense now. I just wish you'd told me the truth."

"I couldn't do that Jennifer. I'm sorry you got hurt, but I just couldn't tell you what was really going on."

"I understand. I'm not blind. I've seen what's been going on. You don't deserve all that."

"Except with Laura, I deserve that and more."

"Probably." she said.

"I just wish everyone could understand. They have all these ideas about what gay guys are like, all these stupid stereotypes that they pin on me and Tay, and they just aren't true." I felt myself opening up to Jennifer. She was the last person in the world I ever thought I'd be talking to about such things, but she was an attentive listener and I guess I just needed to talk to someone about it.

"Well, I don't fully understand myself. I mean, aren't you guys supposed to like dressing like women? I can't picture you in a dress!"

"That's just it. Everyone has all these stupid ideas. I'm sure some gay guys do dress like that, but I don't, Tay doesn't, and I bet most homosexuals don't. I wish everyone would get that crap out of their heads and just look at what I am. I feel like I need to explain to everyone I meet now that I don't want to be a woman, I don't molest little kids, I don't want every guy I see, and all that."

Jennifer was listening to me quietly. I went on.

"I'm the same guy I was before everyone found out about me and Tay. I love soccer, and running, and rock music, and hanging out with my friends. I love fast cars, roller-blading, mountain biking, motorcycles, cheese burgers, pizza, and a good buzz from beer. The only difference between me and the guys that put me down is that I'm attracted to guys. Why should that even matter to them? I could understand if I put the moves on them or something, but I haven't done shit to those guys. Why should my sexual preference be any more important that what flavor of ice cream I like, what kind of music I listen to, or what I like on my pizza? Why does it have to be such a big deal?"

I was ranting. I looked at Jennifer.

"I'm sorry."

"It's okay Mark. I kind of understand how you feel. You aren't any different than you were. Actually, I think it's cool that you and Tay are going together.

You're cute together. Sure, I'd rather you were going with me, but I understand why you can't do that."

"Thanks Jennifer." I really meant it and she could tell. "You know, I'd really like for us to be friends, now that you know I can't be your boyfriend."

"I'd like that Mark. I've always liked you and I'm not just talking about the way you look without a shirt." She smiled wickedly. "Besides, as your friend, I can still look." I laughed.

"You know Mark, those guys should be glad you're gay."

"Huh?" I said, confused.

"Well, if guys as hot as you and Tay are gay, that lessens the competition. Look at me. I can't have you, so now I'll have to pick one of them. If you weren't gay, they wouldn't have a chance." Jennifer was smiling. She was kidding, but she was serious too. I guess it did make sense. Regardless, it made me feel pretty good.

We kept walking, and talking. It felt good to have a friend, especially one that was so unexpected. First Steve, then Jennifer, what other surprises awaited me? It seemed that Taylor and I did have a few friends, not many, but at least not everyone hated us.

17 The Soccer Team

Brandon and Jon had been standing up for Tay and I, but they really showed what great friends there were the weekend after we were outed. Our soccer team was playing in a regional match. We were just one win away from playing in the championship game. Needless to say, everyone was excited about that possibility. We were traveling further than ever, so the whole team would once again be staying overnight in a hotel. It was quite unlike our earlier trip however. That became quite clear very fast. I was about to sit next to Tay on the bus when Coach McFadden yelled at me.

"Mark! Not there! Find another seat tinkerbell!"

The homophobic crowd snickered at that. My face blanched in pain. Coach McFadden had never been a favorite of mine, he was way too obsessed with winning at any cost. He'd been a real jerk ever since my Dad called him and narked me out however. Coach didn't approve of gays. I'm sure he would have kicked both Tay and I off the team if he wasn't so obsessed with winning. Coach knew as well as anyone that without us, the team didn't stand a chance. I know that sounds conceited as hell on my part, but it was true.

I glanced around for a kind face, but most of the guys were avoiding my gaze. The few who were looking at me were openly glaring at me in contempt. Those guys had been riding me and Tay all week, but with the coaches backing, they were bolder than ever. They were like a pack of wolves drawing strength from each other (my apologies to wolves for the comparison). As I walked down the aisle, it was amazing how many of those guys had to cough and how much those coughs sounded like "fairy" and "faggot". I was so humiliated. Knowing that Taylor was witnessing it all made it that much worse.

Such a short time before, I had counted every last one of those guys as friends. We were a team, almost a family. All that had changed, most of them were too uncomfortable to even talk to me, and a few hated me with a vengeance. It had been a very hard week. My nerves were frayed and it was almost more than I could bear.

"Mark, over here." said Brandon, getting up out of his seat.

I smiled my thanks and took his place beside Jon. Brandon dropped into the seat next to Tay. Coach McFadden gave Brandon a glare for that, but Brandon just glared right back at him until coach knocked it off. The Nazi's didn't like it either. They tried staring Brandon down as well, but he shrugged them off. When they discovered he couldn't be cowed they backed off. I tried not to let those guys get to me. I tried to act like it didn't matter, but my heart was breaking inside. Only Jon saw the single tear that ran down my cheek.

Jon was a real friend. He smiled at me wanly, patted my knee, then plunged into his analysis of our upcoming game. He jerked my mind away from my troubles and onto soccer. Jon knew how much I loved the game, hell, everyone on the team knew. I glanced over at Taylor and he was quietly talking with Brandon. I relaxed, he was in good hands for the moment. We were lucky to have such good friends. I wouldn't forget what those guys had done for us. I know I keep repeating that, but that's how important their friendship was to me. I could repeat it a thousand times and it still wouldn't be enough. One never realizes how important stuff like that is, until it's gone.

Coach didn't play me or Taylor during the entire first half. During every preceding game, both of us had been on the field nearly the entire game. Coach only subbed us out when we were ready to drop. That had changed, he subbed everyone else in, but us. I kept waiting for him to call my name, but he never did, not once. Now that coach knew Taylor and I were gay, it changed everything. It seemed he wasn't going to play us at all. I doubted that however. If he wasn't going to use us, he would have kicked us off the team. That's the kind of person he was. Maybe he was just punishing us for being gay.

Our team-mates noticed our lack of game time too. Brandon and Jon were annoyed and angered by it. Devon and his Nazi's smirked in triumph and patted each other on the back for keeping the queers out of their game. Most of the guys just took their places on the field with discomfort. One of them actually apologized to me as he ran onto the field. I know he felt genuinely bad about what was going on, but it made me feel like crap. I did not want to be the object of pity. I was hurt and mad as hell. I looked over at Tay and I could see how upset he was. He knew we were being singled out and he knew why. Seeing his pain deepened my own feelings. I was cut to the quick, and furious at the same time.

Coach was hurting the entire team just to get at me and Taylor. By half-time, we were down 3-0. The team we were playing wasn't even all that tough! The Trojans had a reputation as a hard team to beat, but what I saw on the field didn't impress me all that much. I don't mean to sound conceited, but Tay and I were both kick ass players and our team would have been in the lead if coach had played us.

Brandon and Jon were complaining loudly for him to do just that. A few of the "neutrals" were beginning to murmur as well. Things were getting ugly on the bench and the field. I felt responsible for a few moments, but it wasn't my fault. It was coach who couldn't deal with my sexuality. It was his problem and he was inflicting it on the entire team. Still, being at the center of yet another conflict made me sick to my stomach. I looked at coach in disgust. That was what he was after. He was intentionally trying to hurt me and Taylor. He knew that when he put us in, we'd win the game for him. He could make us feel like crap, then use us to win.

I was pissed. I had half a mind to refuse to play when he put me in. I didn't want to play for him! But no, it wasn't just coach I'd be hurting, it was the team. True, some of them deserved to be hurt, but most didn't. I wasn't going to sink to coaches level. I'd play and I'd do my damnedest to win. I wouldn't do it for him or the Nazi's. I'd do it for me, Taylor, Brandon, Jon, and all those other guys on the team who didn't hate me because I was different.

The murmuring quickly grew into complaining. The Nazi's didn't like that. It was a show of support for me and Taylor. No, they couldn't have that!

"Guys, quit complaining." said Devon, "We'll kick their asses! We just need to punch up our defense and get aggressive."

"We can't do it without Taylor and Mark." said one of our team-mates who had so far remained silent about the two of us. There were a few muttered, "yea's" from the neutrals. That lit a fire under Devon.

"We don't need the fairies playing on our team! They might get hurt and start crying!" His voice dripped with sarcasm.

"Shut up Devon!" Brandon stalked over to him. He was enraged. I had never seen him that pissed before. His muscled bulged. If Devon had any sense at all he would have shut his mouth.

"No! Why are you always taking up for them? What are you, some kind of faggot lover?"

That was exactly the wrong thing to say. Brandon grabbed Devon by the throat and punched him so hard in the face that at first I thought he'd killed him. Devon hit the dirt, unconscious. Our entire team, our opponents, and most of the crowd just gawked. Coach grabbed Brandon and sat him down on the bench.

"You're out of the game ass hole!" Gee, coach always knew just what to say. I thought Brandon was going to jump up and kick his ass, but he controlled his temper. It was a good thing for coach too, Brandon would have beat the hell out of him if he'd started. Brandon was not someone to fuck with. He was sitting on the bench seething with fury. Devon's buddies were keeping as far away from him as they could and even the neutrals had drawn back. Only Jon dared to draw near.

Coach McFadden and one of the referees carried Devon off to a nurse's station. Devon was out cold. The whole fight had involved only two hits, Brandon hitting Devon and Devon hitting the ground. I covered my face with my hands for a few moments. I couldn't believe what was happening. What had gone wrong with my life? Taylor sat near me, shocked. The mix of emotions on his face was hard to read. He looked like he was so wound up, he was ready to explode.

The second half continued and things went from bad to worse. Our team couldn't make a goal to save their lives. The Trojans ran the score up to 6-0. Coach finally relented and subbed in both Taylor and I. He put Brandon back in as well. He held out as long as he could, but in the end, he had to play us. I was beginning to wonder there for a while. I really thought he might blow his shot at a championship just so we couldn't play. I was right the first time however. The only thing more important to coach than his vendetta against us was winning. Coach had always been obsessed with winning. Nothing was more important to him than that. He'd cheat, lie, scream at his players, do anything it took to win. He did win a lot of games, but he was a loser in my eyes.

I knew coach was just using us, but I was playing for the team, not him. I hadn't been on the field for two minutes before I scored. I was so pumped up with emotion that no one could stop me. Taylor and Brandon seemed to have the same advantage going for them. Before ten minutes passed, they had each scored as well.

The Nazi's were still up to their old tricks. They wouldn't even pass the ball to Taylor or me. What a bunch of shit heads. We didn't need them however. Everyone else was working together like crazy to win.

With thirty-four seconds to go we tied up the game. Our opponents headed for our goal, seeking a win. I swiped the ball from an astonished Trojan and booted it down field. Tay zipped in and captured it before our opponents could kick it back. The clock ran down as we jockeyed for position. Our opponents were fierce in their defense. There were no openings anywhere. We were passing like crazy, but to no avail. Brandon booted the ball back to me, but there was just no way I could kick for a goal. Tay broke into the open for a split second. I shot the ball to him and, just before the whistle, he fired it into the goal.

Our team went crazy, the Trojans were crushed. I looked over at coach. He was elated with the win, but he was intentionally ignoring Tay. He didn't want to give him credit for the winning goal. Brandon, Taylor, and I had saved his sorry ass, but I knew we'd never hear a word of thanks or encouragement from him. Devon's little crew actually looked pissed that Tay had made the winning goal. The hatred those guys had for us was un-real. Without us, they would have lost. There was no way they couldn't have realized that, and yet they scowled at us in anger. They just couldn't give it up, not even for a few minutes.

We piled in the bus for the short ride to our hotel. To offset our bit of well-earned happiness, Devon's crew toiled at making our lives a living hell. Devon stepped onto the bus with a major bruise on his face. There was hatred in his eyes when he looked at Brandon, but he didn't dare say a word. He'd learned his lesson. His fear of Brandon didn't stop him from leaning over and whispering in my ear however.

"I'm gonna get you fuckers, just you wait." he hissed like some wild lunatic. He shouldered me as he went on and sat with his little group of followers. They whispered, looked at Tay and I, and laughed. I never could hear what they were saying, but they made it clear that they were cutting us down. I tried to ignore them and talk to Jon, but they were hard to ignore. I noticed Tay was having the same problem sitting with Brandon.

I was assigned to room with Brandon, and Taylor was put in with Jon. It wasn't what either Taylor or I wanted, but we knew for sure coach wouldn't put us together. Yeah, that was going to happen! Still, it was much better than it could have been. We could have been assigned to room with one of Devon's Nazi's. Now that would have been a riot.

After supper, Brandon and I settled in and watched some TV. Brandon pulled off his shirt and made himself comfortable. His torso rippled with hard muscle. Brandon was strong. I was glad he was on my side. He noticed me looking at him, but instead of freaking out and being all worried over whether or not I was checking him out, he asked me something that surprised me.

"Mark, how do you think I look? I mean, you're attracted to guys and all that. What do you think of me? What do you think the girls think?"

"Well," I paused, it was a little awkward. "Honestly, I think you're hot. You've got a great body, cool hair, and you're exceptionally good looking. You're damned nice too and you're not stuck on yourself. That's makes you extremely attractive. I'm sure the girls see you the same way."

"Thanks." he said. I could tell he really meant it. It was wonderful to have someone who could be so comfortable around me. Brandon didn't give a damn that I was gay, anymore than he cared what television show I liked best. My sexual orientation was just another part of me. He was my friend and he accepted me as I was, all of me.

"Thanks for sticking up for me and Tay. We don't have many friends these days."

"Don't mention it Mark. Those faggots...." Brandon stopped in mid-sentence. He looked at me. Pain and embarrassment were etched on his face. "I'm sorry Mark, I didn't mean..."

"Brandon, I understand. Everyone uses that term without thinking. Hell, I even have. I can't say I like it, or that it doesn't hurt sometimes, but it's just the way it is."

"I am sorry." said Brandon, then picked up where he left off. "Anyway, those bastards shouldn't be allowed to get away with that shit. When Devon started talking shit I just couldn't take it anymore. You guys shouldn't have to put up with that. You aren't hurting anyone and what you do is nobody's business but your own."

"I do appreciate what you did." I said. "It really means a lot to me, and I'm sure it does to Taylor as well. I won't forget it."

"You're going to embarrass me if you keep talking like this!" laughed Brandon.

"Okay, I'll stop, but thanks."

"Ahhhhhhhhhhhhhh! Stop it!"

It was great to joke around with another guy, without him acting like I was checking him out or trying to get into his pants. With Brandon, I could just be me.

"Mark," Brandon said slowly. "When did you, did you first know? Know you were attracted to guys I mean?"

I thought for a few moments.

"It's hard to say really. I mean, it's been pretty definite for a couple of years, but I'm not sure when I really knew. I'm sure I've always been attracted to other guys, but I'm not sure when I realized it. I mean, all guys admire other guys to some extent. It's hard to say when I realized that my feelings went further, you know?"

"It must be really hard for you." he said.

"You have no idea! Even before all this happened, it was so difficult. I mean, I just felt so different from everyone else. I mean, I was like all the other guys, but I wasn't. Ah, it's just too hard to explain. You'd have to experience it to understand."

Brandon looked thoughtful. I could tell something else was on his mind.

"Mark, if a guy did something with another guy, just once, would that make him gay?" I could tell Brandon was really concerned with what he was asking me about.

"What do you mean?"

"Promise me you won't tell anyone else this okay? Not even Taylor."

"I promise." I said. The room was silent. It was a long time before Brandon spoke. It was clear that he was having great difficulty forcing the words out.

"A couple of years ago. One of my friends was over and we were wrestling around. We both got kind of excited and he noticed my shorts were kind of bulged out, you know."

"Yeah."

"Well, he dared me to take it out and show it to him. It was kind of exciting, forbidden, so I said okay, if he'd pull out his too. We did it. He reached over and well, you know."

I nodded.

"Well," Brandon paused for a moment. "I did the same to him until we both, you know. Does that mean I'm gay?"

"Did you guys do anything else, then or later?"

"No."

"You ever done anything with any other guy?"

"No."

"Ever think about it, or dream about it?"

"Nope, it was just a one time thing. It just kind of happened. It felt good, so we did it. I liked it."

"Brandon, you're not gay, believe me. You just experimented with another guy. I think a lot of guys do that, although most wouldn't admit it. If you were gay you'd be thinking about doing stuff with guys all the time. Besides, I happen to know you're girl crazy. I don't think you could get any further from being gay!" Brandon smiled.

"I've always wondered. I mean, I've never thought I was gay, but still. Thanks Mark." He smiled.

I was glad to be able to help out Brandon, but what passed between us wounded me a bit. Why did he have to be so worried about whether or not he was gay? It was like being gay was some kind of disease or something and Brandon was afraid he'd caught it. He was far more accepting than others, but the fear of it was still there. I pulled my mind away from being hurt. Brandon was a good friend, one of a rare few, and no one was perfect. I sure as hell wasn't.

Brandon looked at his watch. He got up and walked to the door.

"Come on." he said.

"Where?"

"Just come on."

I slipped on my shoes and followed. He led me to Taylor and Jon's room. He softly knocked and we entered.

"You ready?" said Brandon.

"Just let me get my tooth brush." answered Jon. He grabbed it and went to the door.

"Goodnight guys" said Brandon.

"I'll be back in the morning before coach comes around to wake us." said Jon. With that, our two buddies disappeared, leaving Taylor and I alone. Tay looked as surprised as I was. It was as wonderful as it was unexpected. Brandon and Jon really were great friends.

I was thrilled, but it was clear that something was really wrong with Tay. He ran to me and wrapped his arms around me.

"Hold me Mark."

I hugged him tight and he started crying, not just a little either. It was like a damn had burst. I held him tight and ran my fingers through his hair.

"It's going to be okay Taylor. We'll get through all this. You'll see."

With that, he cried harder still. His tears soaked my shirt. I just held him close and tired to comfort him. Pretty soon, I was crying too. The whole week really had been too much. My nerves were frayed and I felt so very insecure. I was holding up much better than Tay and I was on the verge of a breakdown. What must it have been like for him? He was so sensitive. Taylor was eighteen, but in some ways, he was still very much a little boy.

I held him and gently swayed back and forth. I would have done anything to make everything okay. I loved him so much it hurt. I felt his pain more keenly than my own. After a long while, Tay stopped crying. He led me to the bed and we sat on the edge. He gazed at the floor, more depressed and upset than I'd ever seen him.

"Tay, it will be okay. You'll see."

"It won't you know!" he said earnestly, turning to me and peering at me with his bright eyes. "I love you Mark, and I appreciate what you're trying to do, but you know as well as I do that it's not going to be okay. It will never be okay!"

"Tay." I reached out and grasped his chin. He pushed my hand away.

"It's always going to be like this, or worse! You've seen how they look at us! How they treat us! The things they say!" Taylor was fighting hard not to start crying again. "They hate us Mark! I can't take it anymore! It's too much! People who I thought were my friends! My own parents! I just can't handle it!"

"Not everyone is like that." I said.

"Yeah, but most are Mark, most are! Someone put a note in my locker, you know what it said?"

I shook my head "no".

"It said," Tay halted for a moment. I could tell he was using every ounce of control he had not to cry. "It said, 'I hope you die and burn in hell fag!'" Taylor started crying again and I pulled him to me once more.

Taylor rocked back and forth on the bed. He was bawling and shaking. He was really scaring me.

"I can't live like this Mark! I just can't! I won't!"

My blood turned to ice to hear those words. I knew he meant it. Taylor was not exaggerating for effect, he really meant it. "God help us" I silently prayed. I held Tay close as he cried, trying to soothe him with words. I don't know if he even heard me. He seemed out of his mind with sorrow and grief. I didn't know how to handle our problems, but handle them I would, somehow. I'd be strong enough for us both.

I finally managed to calm Tay down, at least partially. I grasped his chin and pulled his face to mine. I kissed him. He returned my kiss with passion and great hunger, not a physical hunger, not a hunger for sex, but an intense hunger for love, and acceptance. Tay needed to be loved and I did love him, with all my heart. That night, I made love to him with my body as well as my soul. For a few hours, we lost ourselves in each other's embrace. For that brief interval of time, we shut everything out but our love for each other. It was one of the most beautiful nights of my life.

18 From Bad to Worse

Days passed and little improved. If anything, the situation was worse. The stares, the derogatory comments, and the discrimination went on. Teachers stood by and did nothing while my class-mates called me "fag" and "queer". True, some intervened, but most just let it slide, like it was okay to treat someone like that if they were gay. It was as if the laws, rules, and even the very idea of treating others with kindness and respect meant nothing because I was gay. I didn't have the same rights as others because I was attracted to other boys.

A handful of friends stood by me, but their numbers were depressingly low. Most of even my closest friends distanced themselves from me. I was still the same person, but to them I was someone else entirely.

My life was a living hell. I couldn't go for ten minutes without being cut down or finding myself on the receiving end of a hateful stare. I just couldn't get over the idea that some of my class-mates actually hated me. Hate, the real thing! They acted as if I'd killed their best friend or something, and all because I was gay. I tried not to let it get me down, but I failed. Happiness was driven from my life. All I had was Tay.

I was sick with worry over Taylor. I never saw him smile or laugh. His once sparkling eyes were dead. His spirit was crushed by the continual abuse. I guess I couldn't blame him. I was far less sensitive than Tay and I was on the verge of depression. Even the things he once enjoyed didn't snap him out of it. Once, Taylor was a wild boy during soccer practice. He was a terror on the field. All that was gone, he just went through the motions, emotionless, joyless. It was if someone had come along and sucked the life right out of him. It made my heart ache. One of the happiest people I knew couldn't even smile.

I tried to help him, tried to ease his pain, but Tay would not be comforted. Even when he kissed me it wasn't the same. I knew he still loved me, but his heart was heavy. He couldn't break free of the sadness and brutality of his life. I watched helpless as he slipped further and further into darkness. It was like watching someone you love dearly die, a little at a time. I feared for him, wanted desperately to help, but I was powerless.

My own life was little better. My only comfort was Taylor, and he had become not a comfort, but a desperate worry. My own troubles were beating me into the ground and Taylor's problems were crushing my will to fight back. My life hit a new low one afternoon after soccer practice. Taylor was so down he actually walked off the field in the middle of practice. I called to him, but he didn't answer. He just walked away.

My heart wasn't in practice after that, but I stuck it out, as I was sticking it out with my life in general. I lingered on the field before going in for a shower. I knew I wasn't welcome there and I waited for the crowd to clear out. When I finally came in the place was deserted. I showered, then went to the locker room to dress.

I had just pulled on my boxers and shorts when I heard someone enter the locker room. I looked up. It was Devon and three of his Nazi's. The color drained from my face. I wished I was anywhere, but there. Devon smiled at me, but it was a cold, wicked smile, without friendship, steeped in spite and hatred.

"I've been waiting for a chance like this faggot. I told you I was going to get you. I'm going to fuck you up bad."

Devon advanced on me. There was no where to go. He slammed me back against the lockers, his forearm crushing my throat. I couldn't breath. I fought to break free, but two of his buddies each held one of my arms in place, while the third just stood back and laughed at me.

Devon pulled his fist back and doubled me over with a sharp punch to my stomach. As I doubled over, he kneed me in the face, busting my lip, loosening my teeth. I tasted blood. Before I could even begin to recover, he kicked me in the nuts, full force. I screamed in pain and hit the floor. Devon savagely kicked me in the ribs.

"Stand up fucker! Get up faggot so I can give you some more!" He kept kicking me. I thought I'd pass out from the pain. I wanted to do so desperately. It was unbearable. Devon's buddies pulled me to my feet. They had to hold me upright. I couldn't stand on my own. My head was spinning, my stomach felt like it had been ripped apart, my balls felt like they were crushed.

"Beg me to stop fag, and maybe I will. Beg me!"

I looked into his eyes, my own filled with scorn. I'd never beg him, no matter what he did to me. I'd never give him the pleasure of hearing me beg. My eyes were filled with hate and defiance. I knew he'd make me pay for it, but I didn't care, I'd never bow down to him. He could beat me, beat me to death, but I'd never humiliate myself in front of him. My defiance infuriated him. Devon didn't just want to hurt me, he wanted to break me. Never.

Devon punched me. His fist smashed into my face, my stomach, my chest, my nuts. He hit me again and again in his fury. I struggled to get away. I'd have done anything to get away, but my body wouldn't function. I couldn't begin to break free of the hold Devon's buddies had on me. My strength drained away. The searing pain made it impossible to even stand. Devon grabbed me by the chin and spit into my face.

"I should just kill you faggot! Then there'd be one less of you."

I didn't say anything. It wasn't just defiance anymore. I couldn't speak, I couldn't make my mouth function. I couldn't think. My vision was blurred, my mind clouded by pain. I really thought Devon was going to kill me. I really thought I was going to die. It didn't seem like such a bad thing. If only I could escape from the pain. The only reason I wanted to live was so that Devon wouldn't have the pleasure of watching me die.

Devon slugged me once again in the face and his buddies let me fall to the floor. They stood around me, kicking me savagely while they cussed at me and told me I didn't deserve to live. When they stopped, I lay face down on the floor, my body broken and bloody. Devon pulled my head up by the hair.

"You tell anyone about this and I'll kill you faggot. I promise you I will. I'll kill you and your faggot boyfriend."

He smashed my face into the floor. I went out cold and remembered nothing more.

I awoke in the emergency room, with no idea how much time had passed, or how I got there. I was in a daze. My head hurt, my face hurt, my nuts hurt. Hell, everything hurt. Faces swirled in and out. Doctors, nurses, my mother's, Brandon's, Jon's, and others. I'm not even sure if they were really all there. My head swam in pain. I couldn't focus, couldn't think. I wasn't even sure I was really there. The only thing I was certain about was that I had never felt so bad before. I felt like I'd been hit by a truck, a big one.

My first lucid thought was the next morning, at least I think it was the next morning, when I awoke in a hospital room. I was bandaged, bruised, sore as hell, but apparently whole. Tubes ran to my arms and up my nose. I had no idea how I'd gotten there. The last twenty four hours were all a blur. I felt a hand on my forehead, it was Taylor.

"Tay." I said. The weakness of my own voice surprised me.

Tay took my hand, there were tears in his eyes.

"How do you feel?"

"Like Mrs. Simpson sat on me, repeatedly."

Tay smiled at my attempted joke. Mrs. Simpson was our Algebra teacher and weighed well over 300 pounds.

"Shouldn't you be at school Tay?" It was mid-morning.

"I skipped. You think I'm going to leave you here alone when you need me? I didn't find out about what happened to you until this morning when I got to school. Everyone's talking about it."

"Gee, everyone talking about me, what a novelty." I'd been the talk of the school so often it would have felt strange if I wasn't. "How did they find out anyway?"

"I don't know, but you know how stuff like this gets around."

"No shit!" I coughed, it was hard to speak.

Taylor spent the next hour trying to cheer me up. Our roles were reversed. For days I'd been trying to break Tay out of his depression, now he was trying to make me feel better. My pain was mainly physical however, and would heal sooner or later. Taylor's was much deeper and much harder to overcome. Who knew that better than I? I was almost glad to be stuck in that hospital bed. At least it meant I didn't have to return to school.

The days before I was outed seemed almost a dream. I was a star soccer player and had the admiration of my peers. I could walk down the halls without anyone bothering me. Girls thought I was cute and pursued me. Even though I wasn't interested in them, it sure made me feel good that they wanted me. Hell, even my "girlfriend's" mother was after me. I know everything was far from perfect then, but looking back it seemed like a golden age. At least then my life wasn't a living hell.

"Who did this to you Mark?"

"Huh? Oh." My thoughts were drifting and it took me a moment to focus on Taylor's question. I think they had me on some kind of pain killers or something.

"Devon," I said. "with Alex and Jeremy. Rob was there too, but he mainly just watched, until they all beat me at the end." I told Tay all I could remember about what happened. My mind was a bit foggy, but I'd never forget what they'd done to me. When I was finished, Tay was trembling with fury, tears rolled down his cheeks.

"I'll kill every one of those fucking bastards! I will!" hissed Taylor.

Tay scared the shit out of me. He meant it. He really did. He actually started walking out the door. I knew that if I let him leave he really would kill them, or get killed himself.

"Tay!" I called. "Please, come back!" My voice cracked.

Taylor turned on his heel and came back to the side of my bed.

"Please, don't." I pleaded with him.

"I'm going to kill those fuckers!" He seethed with fury.

It was terrifying to see him transformed like that. His sensitive, angelic face was contorted by hate and rage. Such fury on the face of one so kind and loving was disconcerting.

"Taylor, look at me!" He stared into my eyes. What I read there filled me with dread. "I don't want you going near them. Promise me you won't."

He didn't speak, just slowly shook his head "no". The hate and bitterness in his eyes was terrifying.

"Taylor, if you love me, promise me. Promise me!"

I was crying. I'd never been so scared in all my life. I was deathly afraid Taylor was going to go out and get himself killed. If not that, he'd kill those boys and spend his life in prison. My flesh crawled with thoughts of what would happen to him there. I couldn't bear it.

"Promise me!" The desperation and despair in my voice was clear. I reached up and grabbed his hand. Taylor looked at me, tears flooding his eyes. At last he relented.

"I promise."

I bawled even harder with relief.

"They shouldn't be able to get away with what they did. Someone should pay them back for it." said Taylor quietly.

"Maybe someday someone will, but I don't want it to be you, understand?"

Tay nodded. He leaned over and kissed my forehead.

"For you." he said.

Taylor came back and visited me every single day. As soon as school was out, he was by my side and didn't leave until the nurses forced him out. It was such a comfort to feel so loved. I sure as hell wasn't getting love from anywhere else.

In the evening of the second day my mother stopped in to check on me. Tay was just heading out to get something to eat. My mom looked at him with dis-'approval. Tay ignored her. Once my mom thought Tay was the most wonderful boy in the world, but as soon as she discovered we were lovers, she did a complete turn around. I waited for her to say something about him, but she didn't. It was just as well. It would only have caused an argument. I was damn well going to have him in my room. My mother looked at me with sorrow and disappointment.

"Mark, how can you put yourself through all this? Isn't it time to give it up? You could find a nice girl, you could..."

"Mother, for God's sake!"

She still didn't understand. She seemed to think that being attracted to members of my own sex was a choice, like I could switch my sexual orientation with as much ease as I could turn the channel on the television. Hell, she acted like my getting beat up was my fault!

"This is what I am. This is who I am. Nothing is going to change. Can't you understand that?"

I looked into her eyes. It was clear that she really couldn't understand. Despite everything, I felt sorry for her. She just couldn't grasp the fact that I was gay. She just couldn't accept it, or comprehend it. At least she cared enough to come and check on me. My dad never visited me, not once. I'm sure he thought I got what I deserved. Hell, he would have probably helped Devon and his Nazi's beat me up.

My mom just looked at me with sorrow, shaking her head. She didn't stay long, and she didn't come back. I wasn't alone however. Tay was there every second he was away from school. Brandon, Jon, and some of the other guys came to see me too. Jennifer was there almost every afternoon. I didn't have many friends, but those I had were good ones.

19 The Graymoor Mansion

I walked down the familiar halls of school. My face was badly bruised, I limped, and my lower lip and left eyebrow had stitches. It hadn't been that long since I'd gotten my stitches taken out from my fight with Steve, and there I was with more of them. I was still sore, but I could get around pretty good. Nothing had really been broken, although I had a couple of cracked ribs and had to wear damned bandages around my lower chest. I'm sure Devon and his buddies were sorry I didn't have any broken bones.

I drew a lot of stares in the halls, but what the hell was new about that? Instead of gossiping about the fag, all my class-mates whispered about the fag that got his ass kicked. I felt no shame in that. How was I supposed to fight off four guys? Any one of them I could have handled. Hell, I might have done okay with two, but not four. I never had a chance. Those bastards taunted me about being weak. They called me "prissy". What were they when they needed to gang up on me like that?

Life at school was still an ordeal. Brandon, Jon and a few others tried to help out both Taylor and myself, but I still felt distinctly unwelcome and unwanted. I can't begin to describe how much it hurts to walk down the halls knowing that most of your class-mates look down upon you and think of you as some kind of perversion. I even caught a few looks of pity here and there. I hated that! They thought so little of me that they actually pitied me! It was beyond belief.

Taylor's disposition had not improved. He had pulled himself out of his depression to be there for me, but he had returned to his downcast mood. If anything, he was down more than ever. I know that the beating I took had a demoralizing effect on him. It was another part of his world becoming unstable and insecure. Tay knew I'd always be there for him, but what had happened brought the point home that someday I might not be there. Those guys could have killed me. They came pretty close. The thought of losing me like that seemed to drive Taylor closer to the edge. There wasn't much I could do about that. I couldn't promise him not to die, or not to get beat up. More than likely, I would get beat up again. I was sure that Devon and his buds were just itching to finish the job. I couldn't avoid stuff like that, it had become a part of my life.

I was more worried about Tay than ever. He was slipping into depression and I couldn't snap him out of it, no matter how hard I tried. We were both off the soccer team and that didn't help. I was in no condition to play and had no intention of playing with the guys who had worked me over. Tay never went back after he found out what Devon and his buddies had done to me. I think he couldn't stand to look at them. He'd made me a promise not to go after them and he'd keep it, but I think he knew that seeing them would be too great a temptation. Sure, we both saw them in the halls at school, but it wasn't the same. He knew that if he was with them in the locker room, something would happen. He wouldn't be able to keep himself from laying into them.

Devon and his crew still glared at me, but I glared right back. I wasn't about to let those son's of bitches think they'd cowed me by working me over. Perhaps they thought I was scared of them however. I never told anyone but Tay who beat me up. I wasn't afraid of Devon's threat to kill me and Taylor, but I didn't think informing on them would solve anything. The school would just look it over and probably feel the same as my dad, that I had deserved what I got. Mr. Montgomery sure as hell didn't do anything to Randy when we got into it. I was the only one who got punished. I knew he'd just tell me it was all my fault and not do a damn thing to Devon or his buddies.

The truth is, I just didn't want to deal with it. I had more than enough unpleasantness in my life without adding more. In the back of my mind I guess I was a little afraid of Devon's threat, not where it concerned me, but I did worry about Taylor. What if Devon and his buddies went after my boyfriend? I couldn't bear to think of them hurting Tay like that. I wouldn't let them. I watched over Taylor. If they wanted to hurt him, they'd have to kill me first.

Taylor and I met almost nightly at the old Graymoor place. I was growing accustomed to that creepy old mansion. It was almost like it was our home. It was dark, dusty, and dilapidated, but no one bothered us there. It was the only place we could be together without eyes peering at us. It was the only place we could be alone, and hold each other close. If there were ghosts there, they didn't trouble us. That old haunted house was the only place we felt welcome.

Taylor was really depressed, except when I held him. When I wrapped my arms around him it was like he could feel how much I loved him. I think he felt safe, like nothing could hurt him, as long as I held him in my arms. I wished I could hold him forever and protect him from the entire world.

The old mansion was our sanctuary, it was our world. There we talked, and hugged, and made out. There we made love to each other. It was odd. I'd always been afraid of that old house, but I actually looked forward to going there each night. It was our place, mine and Taylor's, and that made it special, no matter what had happened there in the past.

We spent a lot of time exploring that old mansion. It was a hazardous pastime. The floors were weak and groaned in protest under our weight. There were a few rooms we couldn't even enter for fear of falling through the floor. The place was a mess, but it had been beautiful once. Everything was just the same as it had been when it was abandoned, almost a century before. As I looked at the once grand furniture and once elegant surroundings, I fantasized that Taylor and I would buy the old house, fix it up, and live there together. It would forever be our sanctuary from the cruel world.

Some nights, we'd leave the old house and walk to the soccer fields. We'd lay there looking up at the stars, just like we did before everyone found out about us. We were always afraid someone would find us there, but we went anyway. I held Tay close as we looked into the heavens. It made me feel a little safer knowing that the stars would always be there. No matter what went on down on earth, the stars remained untouched. They were something special that no one could take away from us.

20 A Short Rest

Our nights alone weren't enough. Taylor was in higher spirits when he was with me, but we couldn't be together all the time. If only we could! I racked my brain to find some way to snap Tay out of his depression. The only thing I could come up with was getting him away from everything, all the stares, taunts, and unkind comments spoken under the breath. Fall break was just a few days away and it would be the perfect opportunity for us to get away. That was it, Tay and I would take a vacation from the cruel world.

For all the trouble it took, you'd have thought I was organizing an expedition to the moon. I was still more or less under house arrest. The only way I could get away was to talk my Aunt Anne into covering for me. I had always been her favorite and she was the one person I could count on. She was the only relative that didn't openly disapprove of my relationship with Tay. She was also the only one who knew there still was a relationship. She was the one family member that hadn't freaked over my being gay.

Aunt Anne was always cool. What's more, I knew she didn't approve of the way my parents were treating me. She'd visited once since I was outed and I could tell she did not like how things were one bit.

I was nervous when I called her and explained my plans. I told her about what was going on with Tay and how worried I was about him. Thankfully she agreed to go along with it all. Good old Aunt Anne!

I went downstairs to the kitchen and just a few minutes later Aunt Anne called. My parents had a speaker phone and I could hear everything. Aunt Anne asked if I could stay with her during fall break. She told my parents that she thought I might want to get out of the city and that she could use a little help installing her new kitchen range and painting the barn. The last part was a nice touch. Aunt Anne lived alone and my parents weren't likely to deny her my presence if they thought she needed help. I was right, I had my vacation.

The next step was to free up Tay. I called him and explained everything, then Brandon, and pretty soon Brandon was calling Tay and talking to Tay's mom. Tay called me, it was all set. Taylor would be "spending a few days" with Brandon. In reality, he would be at Aunt Anne's with me and Brandon would cover for him. Gee, when did my life become so complicated?

We had Wednesday after school through Sunday for fall break. Unfortunately, Taylor could only stay from Wednesday night until Saturday, but I wasn't about to complain about that. Three days with Taylor was more than I'd ever had.

Mom drove me out to Aunt Anne's on Wednesday, just after school. I suggested that I drive myself, as it was a three hour drive one way. My parents wouldn't hear of it however. I was still denied the use of a car. My parents were terrified that I'd try to see Taylor. Little did they know that I was going to be spending three whole days with him!

When we arrived, Mom started chatting with Aunt Anne and showed no signs of leaving anytime soon. The longer they talked, the more nervous I became. Brandon and Taylor were supposed to show up around eight and the minutes were ticking away. What was I going to do if Mom was still there when they arrived? My three days with Taylor would be over before they started. I'd get Aunt Anne in trouble too. I wasn't good at the whole dishonesty thing. It took too much planning. I hadn't considered that mom would stick around after we got there, although I should have known she would.

To my considerable relief, Mom departed for home at ten till eight. Brandon showed up with Tay about twenty minutes after that. Everything worked out well in the end, but I was sweating it.

Aunt Anne invited Brandon to stay for supper and he gratefully accepted. Aunt Anne makes the world's finest fried chicken and mashed potatoes and all the world seemed to know it.

Aunt Anne really did have a new kitchen range still sitting in it's packing crate. Taylor, Brandon, and I had the old range pulled out and the new one set in place in no time at all. While Aunt Anne fixed supper, the three of us carried the old range out and dumped it in the gully, the final resting place for many old appliances. We spent some time exploring the old junk yard with flashlights. It was filled with rusting hulks from long ago. By the time we returned and washed up, supper was ready.

Taylor was smiling. He was even laughing now and then. Both Aunt Anne and Brandon knew how depressed he'd been, and why. Brandon witnessed it first hand and I'd filled Aunt Anne in on all the details over the phone. She was the one person I could talk to about such things. They both seemed almost as happy as I was to see him edging out of his depression. I think seeing Tay smile made me happier than anything ever had in my life. The chicken and mashed potatoes didn't hurt my mood either.

I couldn't get over Aunt Anne. I knew she was pretty accepting of the relationship between Taylor and myself, but she actually spoke openly about it like no one in the world would have thought anything of it.

"Aren't they cute together?" she asked Brandon.

Tay turned red and I have the feeling I did too. I could feel my face getting all warm. I was shocked that my aunt actually said that. Brandon wasn't phased a bit however.

"Yeah, maybe I should go out and get myself a boyfriend. They do look pretty good together. Of course, Taylor looks especially nice." He laughed.

"Hands off!" I said. "Taylor is spoken for, right Tay?"

"Well, I don't know…" said Tay, pretending to look Brandon over. Everyone laughed at that. It was wonderful to see Taylor kidding around, and it was so cool to be in a place when being gay was okay.

"Ha, like Brandon could ever give up girls!" I said. Brandon was a major babe hound. He was born thinking about girls.

"Well, I am kind of seeing someone. I'm going with Jennifer now."

"Jennifer." I said pointedly. Now that was interesting, especially after what had happened between me and her during the hay-ride. No wonder Brandon was so happy. Jennifer was the kind of girl every guy wanted. She was attractive, sexy, fun to be around, and willing. I was sure those two had been screwing each other's brains out. No wonder Brandon looked so relaxed. Brandon was girl crazy and Jennifer was boy crazy. They were a perfect match. I looked at Brandon knowingly and he smiled. He knew exactly what I was thinking.

We continued talking long after the mashed potatoes had disappeared and the last chicken leg was gone. This was what life was supposed to be like. It was a little after eleven before we pushed our chairs away from the table.

"Brandon, are you sure you won't spend the night?" asked Aunt Anne. She'd asked him a couple of times before.

"Thank you for asking, but I need to get back. I'm spending the day with Jennifer tomorrow." He looked at me and grinned. I knew what they'd be doing.

"Be careful driving home dear." said Aunt Anne.

Brandon smiled and promised her he would.

Just before Brandon departed, I pulled him aside and thanked him for all he'd done. In typical Brandon fashion, he told me to think nothing of it. Aunt Anne pressed a bag filled with chocolate chip cookies into his hands as he left. She even kissed him on the cheek. I could tell she appreciated his kindness too.

Taylor and I washed up the dishes. Aunt Anne protested that we were guests, but I know she appreciated it. When we were done, she was sitting in the living room.

"Let me show you boys to your room."

We grabbed our things and followed Aunt Anne upstairs. She slept on the ground floor, but she took us to the big, second floor bedroom at the far end of the house. I noticed that Aunt Anne didn't even pretend to give Tay a separate room. Our room was huge and had a big double bed right in the middle.

"You boys settle in. I'm going to read a little and go to bed. Don't worry about making too much noise. I won't be able to hear a thing downstairs. You can do whatever you want in this house." Wow, she really was open minded.

"Thanks Aunt Anne." I said, giving her a big hug. She had to be the greatest aunt in the world.

Taylor gave her a hug too. She kissed him on the cheek and mussed his blonde hair.

"I can see why Mark feels the way he does about you." she told him. If anyone else had said something like that, I'd have been shocked, but Aunt Anne was a very special person. Her words sure made me feel good. I loved Tay and it made me happy to see someone else appreciate him.

"Good night boys."

"Good night Aunt Anne."

She closed the door behind her and departed. I had a warm glow inside. Tay and I had three entire days together. Brandon would be back for Taylor on Saturday night and I'd be leaving on Sunday night. Three whole days together seemed like an eternity. All our troubles would be waiting for us when we returned, but for a few hours at least, we could be happy together.

I gazed at Taylor. Every time I looked at him, it was just like the very first time I set eyes upon him. He was beautiful, an angel sent from Heaven just for me. He was an angel touched by sadness, and pain, but an angel none-the-less.

Tay was more calm and content than he had been in a long time, and yet, all was not well. His eyes were troubled, his shoulders slightly slumped, and I could read the tension in his body. No one could go through what Tay and I had experienced and remain unchanged. Taylor looked tired and I knew it was a weariness of the soul, rather than of the body.

I understood what he was feeling, no one could understand it more clearly than I. Tay and I were virtually one. From the very beginning of the whole mess, I was determined to tough it out, make it through. But I wasn't so sure anymore. All the hateful stares, verbal abuse, and finally physical abuse was wearing me down. A great weight pushed on me every moment of every day. I was confident and strong by nature. I had never cared much about what others thought of me, but I was being slowly beaten down.

Devon's smirking face appeared in my mind. It aroused my anger and renewed my determination. I was just tired, that's all. I just needed a break. I could make it. Hell, I'd made it so far. How could things get any worse? It wouldn't be that long before Tay and I finished high school, then we'd go away together, somewhere where no one would bother us. I was determined to go on. I wouldn't let them win. I wouldn't give Devon and his Nazi's the satisfaction. I would tough it out. I just wasn't sure how.

The whole ordeal was far harder on Taylor than it was on me. Taylor was more sensitive than I. Where I was a jock, he was a jock with the soul of a poet. He had a soft heart and cared deeply for others. He keenly felt the pain of the world as few others could. I knew that each disapproving glance, each unkind word, touched him more deeply than it did myself. Tay was more easily hurt and so all that had happened hit him much harder. Why did the world have to be so cruel and unjust to one so kind and loving? Tay was the kind of boy that would have been there for anyone in need of a friend, and yet those he would have helped turned on him, all because he dared to love another boy.

Tay was in higher spirits than he had been in many days, but he was far from the bright eyed, happy boy I'd met not so very long before. I was determined to make him that boy again. I was determined to make him happy. I knew our troubles were far from over, but our weekend together would be a calm, peaceful island in a stormy sea. If we could travel from island to island, maybe we could handle the rough voyage in between.

I took Tay in my arms and held him much as one holds a scared puppy. He hugged me tight, seeking out the comfort and security of my embrace. He nuzzled against my cheek and his lips sought out mine. His kiss was sweet, tender, and loving. All those that put us down, disapproved, or hated us didn't know what they were missing. I almost felt sorry for them because they would never have what I had. If only they could have stood where I was standing, they would have understood that loving someone was a very special thing. What did it matter if the one loved was male or female? So long as there was someone to love and to love in return, it didn't matter at all. I loved Tay with all my heart, and he loved me. There could be nothing more precious in all the world.

A few minutes later our clothes lay in a pile on the floor and Tay and I were wrapped in each others arms on the bed. His body was so strong, so firm, and yet soft and yielding. I pulled him to me, seeking out his warmth and the physical contact that made me feel as if we were one. Neither Tay nor I had ever been with another. I had long and desperately craved sex with another young male, but I was glad the chance had not come until I met Taylor. With Tay, I had far more than mere sex, I had love. All that we did with each other was an act of love, a physical manifestation of what we felt for each other.

That night, Taylor and I made slow, passionate love for hours on end. We held nothing back and gave in to all our desires. We experienced many things for the very first time that night, going further than we'd ever gone before. Each was a new and wonderful sensation that we shared together. It was almost beyond comprehension that two souls could give each other that much pleasure. Whatever might come after, we would have one, beautiful night.

21 A Place Where Evil Cannot Come

I awoke late the next morning with Tay at my side. I couldn't think of a better way to awaken. Taylor's young, naked body looked so beautiful in the morning sunlight. His hair caught the light and shone like gold. He was a living work of art. The sight of him filled me with love, and desire. I leaned over and awakened Tay in a way he'd never been awakened before. His moans of pleasure told me when he had left sleep behind.

An hour later, we showered and dressed. We walked down the stairs and into the kitchen. Aunt Anne was just setting out plates stacked high with French toast. Her timing was impeccable. She always seemed to know just when to do everything.

"How'd you boys sleep last night?" she asked.

"Better than ever before." said Taylor, smiling at me. It was clear that his smile was about more than just sleep. It was so good to see him smile.

We gorged ourselves on French toast, soaking in maple syrup with powdered sugar sprinkled on top. We ate and talked with Aunt Anne. She made us feel so much at home. I found myself wishing that she was my mother. Things would have been very different then. Perhaps they would have been too different however. Who knew? If Aunt Anne had been my mother, I probably would have never met Tay. My life would have been empty. There was no need to think about it. Life was filled with one "if only" after another. I knew that I had to deal with the hand life had dealt me, not get lost in what could have been.

"Anything we can help you with Aunt Anne?" I asked.

"No, no. It's a beautiful day and I want you boys to have fun. God knows you deserve it." Her warmth and kindness touched my heart. Here was a truly kind soul.

"Doesn't your barn need painted?" I asked mischievously.

"As a matter of fact, it does." she laughed. "My hired man is coming this afternoon to take care of it."

Mom really would think I'd been working hard. I just knew Aunt Anne would tell her I painted the whole barn by myself.

"You amaze me." I said. She just smiled.

"Mark, why don't you and Taylor take Flair and Fala for a ride? They could use the exercise."

"Awesome!" I said. I loved horses, and riding. I rarely got the chance to ride however.

"Can you ride?" I asked Tay. I was so excited, I'd already risen from my chair.

"Of course I can ride. I do more than just play soccer you know." Taylor smiled for a moment, then his face darkened with the memory of not being on the soccer team any longer. It wouldn't be long before the championship game, and neither of us would be in it. The sadness soon passed however, and the smile was back. There was something special about our weekend, something that couldn't be ruined by all the pain in our lives.

We headed for the barn and saddled up Flair and Fala. They were spirited, yet gentle horses. In minutes Tay and I were riding side by side through the fields beyond the barn. It was a truly fine day, bright and warm. It was all the more enjoyable because it was usually chilly at that time of year. It almost seemed as if summer lingered, just for us. Aunt Anne's farm really was a magical place. Flair and Fala were excited to get out and cantered beneath us. We let them roam wherever they chose. Our destination didn't really matter, it was the journey itself that was important, kind of like life.

Taylor looked so beautiful with his blonde hair flying in the wind. A smile played against his lips, making him more beautiful still. I wasn't exactly looking my best. I was still bandaged and bruised. I resembled an accident victim more than anything else. Looks didn't matter however, what counted was how we felt about each other. True, it was Taylor's handsome face and form that first attracted me, but it was his spirit and heart that kept me by his side. Maybe it was even his spirit that attracted me first. The night we met, his soul seemed to call out to me, beckon me. I'd felt draw to him and not just by his beauty.

One thing was for certain, if Taylor hadn't been beautiful on the inside, his outward appearance would not have mattered. There were plenty of good looking guys out there, but very few that possessed a beautiful soul. Devon was the perfect example. He was an exceptionally attractive young man on the outside, but on the inside he was spiteful, despicable, and hateful. He was handsome in appearance, but repulsive in his actions. His looks might attract, but his personality was sure to repel.

Taylor and I rode for hours, sometimes thundering across the fields at dangerous speeds, sometimes barely moving along. The horses loved it, and so did we. I guided Flair to the little lake near the rear edge of Aunt Anne's farm. The day had turned fine and hot and I was sweating up a storm. I knew the horses were in need of a drink, and a chance to cool off. As we neared the lake, Tay and I dismounted and let Flair and Fala avail themselves of the cool water. They drank long and waded it for a refreshing swim. We let them wander, I knew they would not abandon us.

The water looked cool and inviting. No one was around, so Taylor and I stripped and dove into the gentle blue lake. Taylor popped up near me, his long blonde hair plastered to the sides of his face. We stood in the water, keeping all but our heads submerged. The cool water certainly felt good on my hot skin. I'd swam in the lake several times, but I'd never skinny dipped before. Doing so with Tay awakened my mischievous side and I dove at him, catching him unaware. I lifted him clear of the water and tossed him back in. He disappeared beneath the surface, and popped back up spitting water.

"Oh, that's it! You're dead!" shouted Tay as he came at me.

Taylor was on top of me in a moment, his muscles bulging as he wrestled with me in the water. We laughed as we wrestled, especially when one of us lost his footing and slipped beneath the surface to come up coughing and sputtering. Taylor splashed me in the face with a great wall of water. For that I dunked him under, only to slip and go under myself. Tay thought that was hilarious, so I had to wrestle him down once more. We laughed as we fought. It was one of those moments that made life special. As simple as it was, it was one of those events that one remembered forever. We must have spent nearly an hour wrestling in the lake as Flair and Fala watched us and nibbled on sweet grass.

We left the water and sunned ourselves on the shore. The hot sun felt so good on my naked skin, and it looked so good on Tay's. I just lay there gazing at him as he warmed his backside in the sun. He was a thing of beauty. Taylor had the cutest little butt. It was as firm as the rest of him. I'd noticed in the locker room that his jock-strap didn't even make an indent in his buttocks. On most guys it kind of pushed in, but not on Taylor.

Taylor noticed me watching him and a shy, awkward smile played across his lips. I loved his shyness and modesty. Taylor was one of those who was unaware of his own beauty and it made him all the more attractive. I still couldn't believe someone so incredibly cute was my boyfriend. I know I've went on a lot about Tay's inner beauty, but I didn't fail to recognize how gorgeous he was either. How could one miss something like that?

Taylor was so sweet, kind, and understanding. It made my heart ache to think what our classmates and families were putting him through. At least I could bring him happiness here and there. We'd have to live for that, the good times in between the rough times. Maybe someday we could be together where no one would judge us harshly. The world as a whole seemed to be growing more accepting of such things, if only our friends, families, and Verona, Indiana could do the same.

We arose and dressed. I pulled Tay to me, kissed him, and told him how very much I loved him. It made me feel very warm inside to hear him echo my words. To love is a wonderful thing, to be loved is infinitely more precious.

We rode back to the barn and tended the horses. By the time we finished, the sky had darkened, and evening had come. Tay and I stood leaning on a fence, watching the fire-flies glow in the near and far distance. I remembered how I'd chased them as a little boy and gathered them into a jar, only to release them a few minutes later.

The crickets and cicadas serenaded us with their song, and somewhere in the distance a whippoorwill began it's haunting tune. A bob white chanted it's name to us. A gentle breeze wafted across the fields, carrying with it the scent of clover and new mow hay. I wrapped my arm around Taylor and held him close as we watched the fire-flies, and the stars. It seemed like paradise.

"I wish we could stay here forever and ever." said Taylor softly.

"Me too, just you, me, and Aunt Anne—wouldn't that be wonderful?" My own voice had a dreamy quality.

Taylor smiled at me, leaned over, and kissed my cheek. I held him close as we watched the darkness deepen. The moon rose, it was beautiful night. I was so happy with Taylor at my side. Simply being with him, feeling his warmth, listening to his breath. That was all I really needed. I wished I could freeze time and just stand there with him forever, experiencing an eternity with Tay at my side. Nothing could have been more wonderful than that.

The world seemed such a beautiful place as we stood there together. It seemed an impossibility that evil could exist in a world so wondrous. I knew well it did exist, but, for the moment, it was elsewhere. Aunt Anne's farm seemed almost a magical place where evil could not come. It reminded me of a place I'd once read about in a book. Evil could not enter that place, and there sorrows were healed. Time could not touch it, and beauty never faded. It was almost as if the author had been describing Aunt Anne's farm. I wished again that Tay and I could stay there forever.

After several long minutes, I pulled Taylor to me and kissed him passionately. Every kiss was like the very first, so filled with wonder and love. We each sought to draw the other closer, to become one. Before I'd met Tay, before I'd kissed him for the first time, I was unable to comprehend how intense, how meaningful a simple kiss could be. I'd thought of all sexual matters merely from the perspective of physical pleasure and desire. It had never once occurred to me that there might be something more. The first time I kissed Tay, and again the first time we made love, I discovered that sensual pleasure was the least of the experience. All the rest, which words cannot begin to describe, was infinitely more powerful and wondrous. No one who has not loved, and been loved in return, can begin to understand. I felt truly lucky that I could comprehend.

Making love with Tay was an experience beyond description, but simply kissing him, touching him, being near him filled me with a bliss that I'd never thought possible before. Taylor had opened my eyes to something wondrous beyond imagination. I kissed him passionately. His lips were sweet and warm. Had I died at that moment, I would have considered mine a full life, all because of a kiss.

I held Tay in my arms as our lips met again and again. I wanted nothing more that to just hold him, and be with him. Why did the world hate me so for wanting that? I could not understand.

Our lips parted, we turned and headed for the house. Aunt Anne would be waiting. Warm light glowed from inside the farm house, a friendly, inviting light. I thought to myself how wonderful it would be if Tay and I could get a house like that someday. Who knew, maybe we would buy the old Graymoor place and fix it up. Anything seemed possible at that moment.

Aunt Anne made us what she called her "breakfast supper" of biscuits and gravy, bacon, sausage, and sweet cinnamon rolls. If I stayed with Aunt Anne long I'd be as fat as the cattle. We ate and talked, and ate some more. The old kitchen was so comfortable, with it's ancient furnishings and kerosene lamps. Aunt Anne liked everything to be old fashioned, and I could understand why. There was something about the glow of an oil lamp that electric light just couldn't duplicate. Taylor looked so handsome in the golden glow, but then he always did. I must have thought how handsome he was dozens of times that day and everyday.

After supper, we all went to Aunt Anne's sitting room. It was a comfortable place with two overstuffed sofas and golden oak furniture from another age. An old pump organ stood in one corner, dark and almost ghostly. Aunt Anne kept the lights off that night, and illuminated the room with only candles and lamps. It made me feel like I was far in the past. It kind of reminded me of the old Graymoor place too. That dilapidated old mansion must have been as warm and inviting as Aunt Anne's sitting room once upon a time.

Tay curled up beside me on the sofa was we chatted with Aunt Anne. It felt so good to be close to him, and to be able to be close to him without a disapproving glance. Tay snuggled up against me like a little puppy. Aunt Anne didn't stare with disapproval as so many would. She didn't frown, didn't glare. She smiled, a warm happy smile that showed that our love for each other warmed her heart. If only the rest of the world could have understood. Aunt Anne did, but she seemed the only one. To her, love was love, the details didn't matter. If only everyone could understand that, the world would have been a far better place.

We talked long into the night. Taylor fell asleep with his head on my chest. I absent-mindedly petted him while Aunt Anne and I spoke in quiet voices. She grew silent for a moment, and just sat there looking at us.

"Mark, whatever you do, don't let everyone else ruin what you have with Taylor. I know your life is hard right now, but you're a very lucky boy. Most people go through their entire lives without finding what you have. It's worth more than any money, it's worth more than any thing."

I smiled.

"I know." I said, looking down at Taylor. "Despite everything, I wouldn't give up what I've had with Tay for anything. I've never felt this way before. I just wish everyone could be like you."

"Everyone has their own thoughts and feelings Mark. We're all shaped by our lives and those around us. None of us can help but be what we are."

It was true, but it didn't make things any easier. I wondered why so many of the boys at school hated Tay and I so much. What did they fear from us? What made them perceive that we had wronged them? I could not comprehend, just as they could not understand me.

Our talk drifted on to other topics. Long after, Tay awakened. We bid Aunt Anne good night and dragged our weary tail-ends to bed. The soft comforters and goose down mattress felt so good to my tired body. I mumbled a good night to Taylor and he murmured something back. I feel fast asleep with Tay snuggled up by my side.

22 Acceptance Among Friends

It's a funny thing, but tales of days that are pleasant to experience, aren't very interesting to hear and don't take long to tell, while unpleasant, even dangerous events, make an exciting tale and take a good deal of telling. The next day at Aunt Anne's was one of those enjoyable days that was fun to live, but not much to tell about. We spent the day walking through the fields and forests around Aunt Anne's farm, exploring, laughing, acting wild, and just generally having fun.

That night after supper, Tay and I took an old comforter and walked out to a little hillock far enough from the house that the lights wouldn't bother us. The sky was as clear as crystal. The stars looked so close I felt like I could reach out and touch them. We spread the comforter on the grass and lay down upon it, staring up at the stars.

"Look, there's the Milky Way." said Taylor. "And the Seven Sisters."

I pulled him close and we gazed out at the vastness of space. I'd looked at the stars before, but gazing at them with Tay was different. I could really see them when I was with him. I didn't just see points of light in the sky. I could feel what they really were and truly appreciate their beauty. There were so many beautiful things in the world that most people just didn't see, even though they were right before their eyes.

Taylor shifted around and rested his head on my chest. I idly twirled my fingers through his hair as we explored the heavens.

"Look" I said. "There's a satellite."

"Where?"

"See, the bright object that looks like a planet. It's moving way too fast to be a planet or star, and it's much too high for a plane. See it?"

"Yeah." said Tay. "You're right. I've never seen a satellite before."

We lay there in silence for a good long time, just looking at the stars and enjoying the closeness. I could hear Taylor's soft, quiet breath and feel his head upon my chest. His hair was silky and soft between my fingers. I was always the most happy when I was with Tay. We'd been through a lot, but it was all worth it. I was content.

"Do you think the world will ever change?" asked Taylor. "Do you ever think they'll be a time when boys like us won't have to hide what we are?"

"I hope so." I said. "But I'm not sure. There's always someone just itching to cause trouble and put someone else down. At least there always has been. I'm afraid there will always be guys like Devon around, but I think things will get better. I think little by little people will start to understand. It'll just take a long, long time. And of course, Verona will be the last place on earth it happens."

"That's for sure!" said Taylor laughing grimly.

We kept watching the stars until we grew chilly. Then we stood and I wrapped my arms around Tay and hugged him.

"I'm so lucky to have you." I said. "I love you so much Taylor."

"I love you Mark, and I'm the one who's lucky." He squeezed me tight, then we headed for the house.

Taylor and I undressed and crawled into bed. We'd taken quite a chill in the night air and the comforters felt good and warm. We snuggled up against each other like two little puppies. Tay's naked skin felt so soft against my own. We fell asleep in each other's arms.

When I awakened on Saturday morning, Taylor was holding me close. It felt so good laying in his arms. I smiled. He leaned toward me and pressed his lips to mine. We kissed softly, then more deeply. We made slow, deliberate love, giving each other as much pleasure as was humanly possible. Each time with Taylor was like the very first, filled with love, warmth, and sensual delight.

It was a good two hours later before we made it out of bed. Neither of us was eager to leave our warm nest, or each other. I slipped out of the bed and pulled Taylor along with me. I led him into the bathroom and turned on the shower. When the water was good and warm, we stepped in. The hot water pounded down upon our young, firm bodies. Even though we'd just made love, I couldn't resist kissing Taylor yet again. We necked in the shower, then lathered each other up and rinsed each other off. Two in the shower was so much more fun than one.

We dried and dressed then went downstairs and had a late breakfast. We were starving. The country air and all the strenuous physical activity gave us voracious appetites. I don't think I'd ever been so relaxed, or so content as I was with Taylor that weekend.

Brandon arrived Saturday afternoon and to my delight, Jon was with him. We weren't really expecting Brandon until later, but both Taylor and I were happy to see him. You might have thought we would have considered his early arrival an infringement on our time alone, but we'd had lots of that and Brandon was a good friend. Not only had he stuck up for us both time and time again, but he was making two six hour trips so we could have some time alone together. Besides, Taylor and I could be ourselves in front of Brandon and Jon, they accepted us for what we were.

Taylor and I had planned a bon fire and weenie roast and we were more than happy to have Brandon and Jon join us. Taylor sharpened a couple more roasting sticks while I started the fire. Pretty soon there was a good blaze going. The logs sputtered and hissed. The fragrant smoke smelled of sassafras. I loved the aroma of wood smoke.

Jon couldn't get the hang of sticking a hot dog on a stick to roast it. He mangled his almost beyond recognition. I tried not to laugh, but a loud chortle forced it's way out. It was just too funny.

"Let me help you with that Jon." said Taylor and impaled his hot dog for him. We were all city-boys, but I don't think Jon had ever been out of town. His ignorance of the country was pretty obvious. On our way out to the bon fire, he had stared at the cattle like they were some kind of weird exotic animals. I don't think he'd ever seen such a thing before. At least he seemed pretty good at roasting his hot dog once Taylor put it on the stick for him.

"How's Jennifer?" I asked.

"Nice, very nice." said Brandon meaningfully. Jon picked up on that instantly. He had keen senses when the topic was sex, no matter how veiled.

"You two been, uhm…" Jon's voice trailed off, he didn't know how to ask what he was asking without saying the wrong thing.

"Yes!" said Brandon. "Oh yes!"

"Man!" said Jon, "Am I the only one not getting any around here?"

Taylor and I looked at each other and grinned. Neither Brandon nor Jon failed to pick up on what passed between us.

"I'm afraid so." said Taylor, patting Jon on the back.

"Someday I'm just gonna explode!" yelled Jon.

We all laughed at that, except Jon.

"It's easy for you guys to think it's funny, I'm serious." That just made us laugh harder. It took us quite a while to get ourselves under control.

We roasted hot dogs, gulped sodas, and talked. It was great to spend time with Taylor and my buddies. Aunt Anne's farm really was a magical world where all our troubles were kept at bay.

Jon had an even bigger problem with the marshmallows than he did the hot dogs. He could get them on his stick all right, but each turned into a flaming torch moments after he stuck it in the fire.

"I swear" I said. "We're going to have to sign you up for a remedial marshmallow roasting class. Here. Like this." I demonstrated how to toast the marshmallow a golden brown, without catching it on fire. Even after my fine lesson, he still couldn't get the hang of it.

All too soon, it was time for Taylor and our friends to depart. I wished they could all stay longer, but we'd had a wonderful time. Taylor packed up his things and threw them in Brandon's car. Aunt Anne came out with a big bag of just baked chocolate chip cookies for their trip home. Aunt Anne thought of everything. Brandon smiled, apparently he'd enjoyed the last batch.

I hugged Taylor tight and said "good bye". I even kissed him right in front of Brandon, Jon, and Aunt Anne. I missed him even before the car was out of sight. My heart ached for him, but I knew it would only be a couple of days before we'd see each other again. Still, I felt my heart tug as the car pulled away. Aunt Anne put her hand on my shoulder and led me back inside.

Aunt Anne was so cheerful that my mood was soon much improved. Aunt Anne was always happy. She was one of those that could see the good in everything.

"You really love him very much don't you Mark?" It was more of a statement than a question.

"Yes." I said.

"I can tell. The way you look at him, and the way he looks at you. There aren't many people who find a love like that. You're very lucky."

"I know, but sometimes I don't feel so lucky."

Aunt Anne looked at me with sympathy.

"I know honey. I know." She came over and gave me a hug. I felt so safe in her embrace. I wished yet again that she was my mother. How different everything would have been then.

Aunt Anne and I talked while she made a late supper. Her voice was like a song that eased my heart. I loved Aunt Anne.

Loneliness touched my heart as I climbed into bed that night. The double bed seemed so huge without Tay. Of course, I wasn't thinking much about the bed itself when Tay was there. That thought brought a smile to my lips. I awakened a few times that night, thinking Taylor was still there with me. I missed him. I'd grown accustomed to sleeping with him at my side. My arms ached to hold him close.

I helped Aunt Anne all the next day. There were endless things she needed done that she just couldn't handle by herself. I was glad to keep occupied and to help out Aunt Anne. She had certainly helped me.

Soon it was eight p.m. and mom arrived to take me home. It was another hour before we actually departed. I was getting sleepy. I'd done a lot of work that day and my muscles ached.

I did not want to return to the hard, cruel world, but I couldn't stay with Aunt Anne forever, and besides, Taylor needed me. I gave Aunt Anne a big hug and a kiss on the cheek. I loved her so for all she'd done. She actually had tears in her eyes as we parted. She was the kindest soul I ever met.

It was after midnight when we arrived home. I crawled into bed, but, tired as I was, I tossed and turned all night long. When I did sleep, I had bad dreams. I couldn't remember what they were when I awoke, but my mind and heart were troubled. I felt frightened, and alone.

23 **The Nightmare Becomes Real**

I was almost cheerful the next day as I walked into school. The bad dreams of the night before were only a distant, unpleasant memory. The little vacation Tay and I had taken together had done wonders to improve my disposition. I had certainly needed the break. Most of the improvement came from seeing Taylor happy however. Tay's well-being was far more important to me than my own. When he was happy, I was happy. It was as simple as that. I lived for him.

I steeled myself for the disapproving glares, the vicious taunts, and unkind words - all the things that awaited me behind those doors every day. I never failed to experience a sense of dread as I walked into school. Each day I mentally fortified myself for what was to come.

Nothing could have shielded me from what awaited me on that day however. As unpleasant as all the other days had been, that day was destined to be infinitely more horrible.

As I walked in, all my classmates looked at me. I had grown accustomed to the unwanted attention, but something more was going on. They were all looking at me, some with disapproval and distaste, but many with sadness and pity. There was a pall over the atmosphere, a dread in the air. I looked about confused, and quite suddenly, afraid, afraid as I never had been before.

Jennifer walked up to me, her eyes filled with tears. She placed her hand on my shoulder. My mind reeled in terror and confusion, what could be so wrong?

"I'm so sorry Mark. I..." Jennifer's voice cracked and tears ran down hercheeks. Others drew near. Jon, Ethan, Matt, Jordan, Steve - they were all there and each of them looked at me with such pity and grief that my heart clutched in terror. Even Laura looked at me with sorrow in her heart. I was lost in a crowd of sadness and gloom. Hopelessness filled the air. I looked from face to face, uncomprehending, disoriented, afraid.

"What's happened?" I asked, uncontrolled terror welling within me, as if somehow in my heart I already knew.

"My God," said Jennifer softly, "you don't even know." I had never heard a voice so filled with pity, sadness, and sympathy. It frightened me as nothing had before.

She tried to speak, she tried to tell me, but the words would not come.

Another voice cut through the haze that clouded my mind, a voice cruel and filled with hate, a voice delighting in other's pain.

"He's dead. Taylor's dead. Your boyfriend killed himself last night." said Devon.

I turned to him. His eyes were filled with malice, hate, and an unmasked delight in destroying my entire world. My heart stopped. I froze.

No, it couldn't be true. It was just another dream, a nightmare. I knew that I was awake however, as badly as I wanted all that was happening not to be real. It was a trick then, a horrible, cruel, evil joke. I looked into Jennifer's eyes. Tears ran down her cheeks. I looked from face to face to find many who looked the same. My heart wretched, I tore at my hair, and screamed.

My eyes flooded with tears. I couldn't accept it, but it was all real. He was gone, dead. My Taylor was dead. My mind screamed. How could this have happened? Why? Oh God why? He was so happy with me. We had experienced such joy together at Aunt Anne's. Everything was on the verge of getting better. Why now? Why?

"One down." said Devon.

The entire hallway grew deathly still. Not one of those standing there could believe what they had just heard. My grief turned to uncontrolled rage. I spun on my heel and smashed Devon in the face. My fist snapped his head around. Devon promptly kicked me right in the nuts. The pain was intense, but I ignored it completely. It didn't phase me for a moment. I flew into him, my fists flying, smashing into his face, his stomach, his chest. Devon was bleeding from a busted lip and a cut over his left eye. One of his teeth lay on the floor.

He cowered before me. I reached down and dragged him to his feet. I read the terror in his eyes. He feared for his life, and rightfully so. I punched him once more. There was a loud snap as his jawbone broke. Devon screamed in pain and fell again, clutching his face. I reached out for him again, intent on giving him what he deserved—death.

I felt strong arms on me, holding me back. I fought to escape, but I could not. It was lucky for Devon that our classmates held me. I have no doubt I would have killed him if I could have gotten my hands on him again. I kept struggling, but I could not break the hold they had on me. I was infuriated. I was totally out of control. All I could think about was killing that bastard.

"Mark! Stop it! Calm down!" I looked with wild eyes into a familiar face. It was Brandon. I didn't know when he'd arrived, he hadn't been there before, but he was one of those holding me back. I stopped struggling when I saw him.

My mind was filled with grief and pain. Brandon and the others released me. The crowd parted as I pushed my way out the front door. I stumbled down the steps, crying, blinded by my tears. I nearly fell, someone caught me, steadied me.

"Come with me."

It was Brandon. He led me away from the crowd and into his car. He drove off as I sobbed uncontrollably. I cried for I don't know how long, an hour, two, more? Finally I settled down a bit. Brandon pulled the car to the side of the road and stopped. I looked into his eyes.

"What happened?" I asked him, sobs still racking my voice.

"Mark, I don't think…"

"Tell me! I have to know!"

Brandon looked like a doomed man, heading for the gallows. I knew that he would have rather done anything than tell me what I needed to know. I knew it brought him unbearable pain, but he told me everything. As he spoke, I could see it all in my mind as if I was there.

"Jon and I took Taylor home on Saturday night. On Sunday evening, we picked him up and we all went out for pizza. Everything was fine. He was happier than I'd seen him in a long time. We even took in a movie. We dropped him off at his house a little after nine-thirty. Less than an hour later he showed up at my house however. He was crying and trembling, his eyes were wild. I'd never seen him like that before. Just looking at him scared the hell out of me. I asked him what was wrong. It took him a long time to compose himself enough to be able to talk.

"'They kicked me out!' he cried. 'My parents kicked me out!' I tried to soothe him, but he pulled away from me. He wouldn't let me touch him. He was upset, almost out of his mind. He started bawling again. It was a good, long time before he could stop crying enough to tell me what happened. Even then he was sobbing, struggling to get the words out.

"When he walked up to his house, after Jon and I dropped him off, he found his stuff sitting on the front porch. His dad came out and started yelling at him. He told him he..." Brandon paused. I could tell he didn't want to go on.

"Brandon, please, tell me."

"He told him he didn't want a faggot son. He said he knew that Taylor was still seeing you, that the two of you had been sleeping together. He knew that Taylor had been with you at your aunt's. I don't know how, but he knew. He cussed Taylor out, called him all sorts of terrible things, things a father should never, never say to his son. He grabbed Taylor and punched him right in the face. He would have done more, but Taylor fought him off. His mom was there, all she did was watch. All the neighbors were watching too by then so Taylor's dad threw his things at him and screamed, 'Get out you fucking little queer and don't ever come back!' Then he went inside and slammed the door. Taylor turned and ran all the way to my house. He was really freaked out. I'd never seen anyone look like that before."

"Why didn't he come to me?" I asked sobbing.

"I think he would have, but you weren't back yet."

"My God! If I'd been home I could have saved him!" I was bawling my eyes out. I was freaking out on the spot. "It's my fault!"

"Mark, listen to me!" yelled Brandon, shaking me. "He was more than half out of his mind. If only you could have seen his eyes. They were wild, crazed, I'd never seen Taylor like that before. He looked...insane. He didn't even look like Taylor, but like some nightmarish version of him. He was out of his head Mark. You couldn't have reached him, no one could."

I looked at Brandon with tears running down my cheeks. Each word he spoke was like a dagger in my heart, but I had to hear it. I had to hear it all. I had to know what happened.

"Taylor kept saying how he'd be better off dead. How everyone would be happy then. He really scared me. I knew he was thinking about killing himself. I talked to him, told him that was nonsense. I told him we'd work things out. I told him he could stay with me, and that you'd be back soon. I told him that every-thing would be okay. That just seemed to make him worse. Then, after a little while, he calmed down a bit and asked for a soda. I went down to the kitchen to get him one. When I came back, he was gone.

"I ran out of the house looking for him. I couldn't find him. I called the police and told them what was going on. They sent out patrols looking for him."

"Why didn't you call me?" I asked, my voice almost desperate.

"I did. Your dad answered, said you wouldn't be back until late. I called your Aunt Anne, but you'd already started home. There was just no way to reach you.

"When I couldn't get you, I called Jon and we went out looking for Taylor. We thought we could figure out where he went. We figured we could find him better than anyone else." Brandon suddenly stopped, tears running down his cheeks. He was bawling.

"What happened?" I pressed, forcing out the words between sobs. It was a long time before Brandon could speak again.

"We found him." said Brandon, his voice eerie and barely above a whisper. "We found him on the soccer field." Brandon paused. He was shaking, his eyes were glazed over with grief and the overwhelming sadness of his memory. Tears were rolling down his cheeks and his voice was racked with sobs whenever he started to speak. It was a long while before he could go on. I waited patiently. I knew how hard it was for him. I knew how it was tearing him up inside. I needed to know what happened, and yet, I didn't want to know. Finally, Brandon was able to go on. When he spoke his eyes and voice were distant, like he was speaking to someone who wasn't really there.

"He was leaned up against the soccer goal, his head slumped over. I approached him and spoke his name, but..." Brandon started sobbing all over again. "But he didn't answer. He didn't move." Brandon's voice was racked with sobs and I was crying too. "I reached out and touched him. He was cold. He didn't move. I checked his pulse. It was still. Jon ran and called an ambulance, but it didn't matter. It was too late. He was already dead." Brandon broke down in tears. I wrapped my arms around him and bawled my eyes out too. It was many long, hard minutes before Brandon spoke again.

"The paramedics came. They found the bottle in his jacket. He overdosed on some pills. I don't know what they were, or where he got them. There was nothing they could do. I'm so sorry Mark."

We sat there for a long, long time, stricken with grief. It was all so unreal. It was like it couldn't possibly be true.

My God, Taylor was dead.

I asked Brandon to drive me home. I opened the car door, but hesitated before getting out.

"Brandon, thank you for all you've done, for me, and especially for Tay. I can't tell you how good a friend you've been. Thank you." I leaned over and hugged him tight. I stepped out of the car.

Brandon had a weird look in his eyes. I think in his heart he knew he'd never see me again.

23 The End of the Nightmare

No one was home, no one would be for a long time. I went to my room and cried my eyes out. I couldn't believe he was really dead. I was in shock and grief. I thought my life had been a living hell before, but it was nothing compared to the loss of Tay. My life was destroyed, there was nothing left. Taylor was gone! The only person that I really loved, and that really loved me, was gone!

"Tay, how could you leave me like this? Why Taylor? Why?"

I was out of my mind with grief. I searched through the medicine cabinets, but I didn't know enough to be sure that what was there would kill me. I rifled through my father's dresser drawers. I found it. Hard, cold, and black - his revolver. I searched out the bullets and loaded the gun. I pointed it at my head and began to squeeze the trigger. I stopped myself. There was something I had to do.

I stuffed the revolver into my backpack and tossed it on my bed. I sat at my desk. There, laying on top, was my English homework. I read aloud the quote that I had used to start my essay.

"In fair Verona, where we lay our scene. From ancient grudge, break to new mutiny. Where civil blood makes civil hands unclean. From forth the fatal loins of these two foes, a pair of star crossed lover's take their life. Whose misadventures piteous overthrows, doth with their death bury their parents strife…"

That's as far as I'd made in on my English report, only a few short words copied directly from a tattered paperback. I crumpled the paper into a ball and sent it sailing toward the wastebasket. It dropped in with a satisfying thump. I wouldn't be needing it any more. Like my life, it had become unwanted and without reason for existence.

I'd struggled through Shakespeare, but I had come to understand him only too well. Life was a tragedy. When first I read "Romeo and Juliet", a task I undertook only under duress, I believed his work bore little resemblance to modern existence. Who really gave a damn about a four hundred year old romance? And why didn't Romeo just find some other babe to plow? My eyes had opened since that day however and I had grown. Shakespeare's words began to make sense. After the events of past few weeks, he could well have been telling the story of my own miserable life. "In fair Verona, Indiana, where we lay our scene. From ancient prejudice, break to new mutiny..."

The parallel was only too clear, but my story did not possess the romantic distance of a past age. The memory of what had so recently passed was not yet dulled and blurred by time. Centuries did not separate me from those terrible events. The wounds were not healed, but were still fresh and painful. Salt was yet being heaped upon them, sharpening the pain, intensifying the torment. My recent past was like a sharp stick, jabbing me in the gut, impaling me while I squirmed to escape. There could be no escape for me however, my fate was set.

All was lost. There was just no other way to describe it, everything that I cared about was gone. My mind reeled with sorrow. How could it all have come to this? Why did it have to be this way? Why couldn't those around me have just understood and let me, let us, be?

Recording what had happened would be a time-consuming task, but I possessed the freedom of a doomed man. I had the rest of my life to set down what had happened. I felt an overpowering need to tell my story. I pulled the keyboard of the computer toward me and began my tale. I'd leave an account of what had happened, so maybe some other boy would not meet my fate.

And so I've come full circle. My Taylor is dead, and I'm soon to follow. There is nothing left for me, Taylor was all I cared about. Without him, there is no life. Without him, there is no reason to suffer the slings and arrows of a cruel world, there is no reason to bear the withering glances, the taunts, the disapproval, the hatred, the abuse. There is no reason to exist. The time had come for the vampire to meet his inevitable fate.

"A pair of star crossed lover's take their life...doth with their death bury their parents strife..." Maybe my own death would bring peace to my friends and family, maybe it would teach them a little about acceptance and understanding. I thought of my Aunt Anne, of Brandon, and Jon, of those few who stood by me and helped me on my way. My heart filled with sorrow.

I wrote out notes to Aunt Anne, Brandon, and Jon, thanking them for being there for me, for us. I thanked them for standing by me, and Taylor, when we needed them the most. I told them their kindness and understanding weren't for naught, what they did brought Taylor and I a short span of happiness dearer to me than all the world. A moment with Taylor was worth a life-time. I told them not to cry for me too much. I was going to be with Taylor, and that's all I'd ever wanted. Maybe Tay and I could at last go to that place we dreamed about. I slipped the notes into a large envelope and addressed it to Brandon.

I turned back to my computer and looked one last time at what I had written. Never was there a story filled with more woe. I hit "save" and sent my story to a floppy disk. I put it in the envelope with my notes and sealed it. I'd mail it to Brandon before I did what I had to do.

I opened my window and looked out of it one last time. Evening had already come and the stars were out. I gazed at them, wondering if Taylor could see them too. I was glad that the stars would always be there.

I glanced at my backpack sitting on the bed. It was time to go. It was time to walk to the soccer field one last time. It was time to join Taylor.

The End

9 781583 482063